"The greate
about the greatest j..cnus there ever were"

Legend of
The Friendship Cats

By Walter Browder

with a prologue by Sue Ellen Browder

JUDE PRESS

Ukiah, California

Jude Press
770 Orr Street
Ukiah, California 95482

Publisher's Note: This is a work of fiction. Names, characters, places, and incidents are a product of the author's imagination. Locales and public names are sometimes used for atmospheric purposes. Any resemblance to actual people, living or dead, or to businesses, companies, events, institutions, or locales is completely coincidental.

Book Layout © 2014 BookDesignTemplates.com

Legend of the Friendship Cats/as told to Walter Browder -- 1st ed.
ISBN 978-0-9979876-0-7

This book is affectionately dedicated to
Ethan and Hunter

...the cat has always been a link between the possible and the impossible.

—Roger A. Caras, *A Celebration of Cats*

CONTENTS

Prologue

This is a story only cats could have lived. It is full of surprises. What's more, it's a legend nearly every cat knows and loves, a favorite story that's continually told and retold whenever cats get together. Mother cats frequently tell "The Legend of the Friendship Cats" to their kittens even before they are weaned. Or so I have heard. But to my knowledge, this amazing story, a deeply cherished part of cats' oral tradition, has never been written down--until now.

How did this extraordinary story happen to come into my possession? Well, that in itself makes for a very strange tale. My beloved husband Walter was a poet, a philosopher, and a dreamweaver, an unusual man with a unique gift. Not only could he talk to animals (particularly to cats), but he insisted he could hear cats talking *back* to him. He began writing this story down when we had an orange tabby American Shorthair named Kismet (Kizzy for short). The writing took more than ten years and still the story was not finished until a brown tabby Siberian cat with green eyes rimmed with gold appeared on our doorstep one day and decided to stay. Since our new house guest was male, we simply called him Mr. Cat.

Walter always claimed Mr. Cat and Kizzy were telling him the story, and that's why it was taking him so long to write it. He explained that cats love to dawdle over a good story and when they begin to tell this particular legend, which is part of their most ancient traditions, they refuse to be rushed. I didn't believe Walter for a minute, of course. I thought he was just pretending to work on a book to get out of mowing the lawn. Really, who could believe such a tale? But my beloved husband was such a charming man, so filled with merriment and wonder, I could never stay exasperated with him for long. So as he wrote and rewrote, the pages of his manuscript piled up until he had accumulated forty-three drafts. When you're being entrusted with the secret things of cats, Walter explained, it's important to take your time and make sure you've got the story just right.

The timeless legend was never published, and perhaps that is how it was meant to be. For as all cats know, everything that happens to us in this life is part of a bigger plan than any of us can see or understand. After Walter died, I bundled the thousands of pages he had written over the years into three large cardboard boxes and stashed them in the garage.

Now here comes the mysterious part of the tale that even I wouldn't believe if it hadn't actually happened to me. One night when I was sitting at home alone in my log cabin before a crackling wood fire, my own cat (who was purring softly in my lap) suddenly looked up at me and began telling me the same story! To say I was astounded is putting it mildly. I was so flabbergasted I could not even speak. It was at that moment I realized that, amazing as it sounds, my beloved Walter had been telling me the truth all along: This truly *is* a story that all cats know and love to tell!

The next morning I went into the garage, dug Walter's manuscript out of the three dusty cardboard boxes, and began to pull all the pieces of the tale together. I now present to you what Mr. Cat fondly called "the greatest story ever told about the greatest friends there ever were"--*The Legend of the Friendship Cats*. If it pleases you as much as it pleases me, you may want to read it aloud to your favorite felines, for cats can never get enough of this story, and no matter how many times they've heard it, they love listening to it again and again.

--Sue Ellen Browder, October 1, 2016

CHAPTER ONE

Gathering Under the Lilac

None of us like it much when our comfortable, cozy world gets completely turned upside down. So it was no wonder the cats were distressed.

Whiskie's white whiskers lay plastered flat against his black cheeks in alarm. "My poor Mom! My poor Mom!" he mewed miserably. His black, bristly tail lashed anxiously back and forth like a flicked whip. With Ridley Park in an uproar, Ali Baba's Captain White Whiskers of Effingham ("Whiskie" for short) had taken advantage of the bedlam to escape from his house. He and seven of his cat friends were now gathered in their favorite meeting place under the lilac bush in Mister Backward's side yard--the one the mockingbirds had built a nest in that summer.

"Don't worry, Whiskie," said Sunny, a golden-shaded American Shorthair. "The police will catch those kidnappers. They'll get your Mom back. You'll see."

At least I hope they will, Sunny thought to himself. His tummy hurt. His normally calm American Shorthair mind buzzed with confusion as he again pictured the tragedy he'd witnessed that morning at Whiskie's house. While he and his black Turkish Angora friend were playing happily with their catnip mice, three wicked men crashed through the front door. They grabbed Whiskie's human Mom Edeline and her two children Buffy and Chip. Then – oh, the horror!– they threw them into a black van and roared away up Van Buren Boulevard toward City Center.

"That was an evil way to treat sweet Edeline!" cried BraveHeart, a fawn-and-brown seal point Siamese. Large tears gathered in his sapphire-blue eyes."What if they hurt her?"

"And what about The Show?" Lady Practical moaned softly. A British Shorthair in a brown tabby pattern, she was the only one "practical" enough to mention this second fear on everyone's minds. Edeline was the prime organizer of the annual Christmas Cat Show at the Gardens. Even now in late September, they were all eagerly looking forward to The Show. But with sweet Edeline kidnapped, how could The Show go on? If it couldn't, there would be no rosettes for any of them this Christmas. Winning a rosette is as much fun for a show cat as winning the Little League World Series is for a kid who plays baseball.

"Lady Practical, how can you be so self-centered as to worry about The Show at a dreadful time like this?" scolded Gloriana, a soft-furred Russian Blue. "Whiskie's human Mom has been kidnapped. You understand? Kidnapped!! They've stolen the sweetest Mom in Ridley Park."

Suddenly, Mister Backward's human Mom came to the side door of the large Tudor mansion across the manicured lawn. "Here kitty, kitty, kitty," she called. "As if things weren't awful enough, now my precious Foldie has disappeared. Mister Baaaackwaaaard!"

"I must go to her," Backward mewed, wiggling his well-rounded body to make his way through the crowd.

"No, shhhh. You can't go yet. We need you," Sunny whispered.

They all hunkered down and barely breathed. Finally, Backward's human Mom went back into the house. Everyone sighed with relief.

Collected at last, Sunny rose on his well-rounded paws, a colossus of calm.

"Quiet down, everybody," ordered Brunnhilde from the back. "Sunny's going to speak." Brunnhilde was a brawny, frosty-grey Norwegian Forest Cat, or "Weegie" as they are fondly called. She had jaunty ear tufts of black fur and emerald-green eyes rimmed with gold. Sunny was the rising star among the Ridley Park show cats. Brunnhilde, whose nickname was Hildy, desperately wanted to hear Sunny's thoughts about the theft of a Mom.

Sunny's strong voice soothed them all. "You know that Whiskie's human Mom and her two kittens have been kidnapped. The police are here. Whiskie's human Dad, Sterling, has lots of money, and he's ready to pay any amount to get his family back. Everyone in Ridley Park has stopped by to offer help. And now, as Whiskie's friends, we must do our part, too."

"Hear! Hear!" Hildy boomed in her large Norwegian Forest Cat voice.

"You're right, Sunny. We must do our part," agreed Lady Practical, nodding her brown tabby head.

"But what *is* our part?" asked Duchess HighMind, a snow-white Persian. Calm and sweet-natured with gold eyes, an adorable little snub nose, and a high regal forehead, Duchess was known among the Ridley Park cats as being very brainy.

Sunny's round, green eyes looked sad. *Good question. What is our part?* he thought miserably to himself. *Our adorable moms feed us gourmet food and brush our coats until they're sleek and shiny. They take good care of everything. What can a bunch of weak, helpless, little show cats like us do against three big, mean, powerful men?*

He glanced sorrowfully at his black Turkish Angora friend lying beside him. Whiskie's tail thrashed angrily back and forth. He detested the three cruel thieves.

"I'm just a poor little show cat," Whiskie wailed. Helpless tears welled up in his amber eyes. "I know nothing of fighting or derring-do stuff.

Then his black ears suddenly perked up. "But I could keep my Mom and her kittens company. I could comfort them. They just love to hear me purr."

The Duchess impatiently tossed her regal, glossy, white mane. Being the intellectual sort, she didn't believe in building castles in the air. "They left in *a van.* You understand? They could be miles from here. How can you comfort them? You can't even find them."

"What about psi-trailing?" Whiskie offered. "I could do that."

"Pish! Psi-trailing, indeed!"

They all knew Whiskie could read his Mom's mind. All cats can tell when their human moms feel depressed or are about to leave the house for the weekend. But psi-trailing is a deep, mysterious talent, a great gift that goes way beyond mind-reading. Could Whiskie really have the gift? They all regarded their black friend with curious, wondering eyes.

Thinking aloud for them all, Sunny said, "Some cats who've been lost hundreds of miles from home *can* find their way home again. And we've all heard stories about cats – a special few who love their moms very, very much–who can journey thousands of miles and find moms who've moved to *new* homes. Maybe Whiskie has the gift. Maybe he *can* find his Mom by psi-trailing."

"Myths and legends," caustically returned the realist. "Stories for kittens in the nest."

But Whiskie was young and full of hope. "There's more to psi-trailing than superstition, Duchess HighMind. What if my Mom's sad and alone? What if those wicked men hurt her? I have to try to find her. I just have to."

"And what about that dream Whiskie had, Duchess? What about that?" BraveHeart chimed in.

They all remembered the dream – and what the fire cat had said. Whiskie had been sound asleep in his favorite chair next to the fireplace. Suddenly, he dreamed that down the chimney came a big, noisy wind, roaring like a king cat. In the dream, Whiskie leaped to his feet and arched his back. All the hairs on his silky black coat stood straight on end as he stared into the fireplace.

There among the andirons and ashes stood a cat made of fire, burning and crackling. Engulfed in flames, the fire cat looked directly at Whiskie and said, "You need a savvy cat like me. And I still owe you."

Then he gave that reassuring blink all cats give when everything's fine. He blinked his copper-colored eyes and held them closed just long enough to say, "Everything's copasetic" (which means "okay" or "hunky-dory"). Then he slowly opened his eyes again.

They had all heard this dream, and they remembered the fire cat's words: "You need a savvy cat like me. And I still owe you," the fire cat had said.

Sunny wisely nodded his golden head and regarded Whiskie with respect. Finally, he spoke. "A cat who can have such a dream, Whiskie, could have a great psi-trailing gift, indeed."

Whenever cats talk over a problem, they talk nonstop until they've said all that needs to be said. Then they sit silently for hours. Eventually, their hearts begin beating in unison, and everything is settled. Now Sunny and his friends stopped talking and huddled together under the lilac bush for a very long time, until late afternoon and evening had passed and late night had come on. When all the stars filled the heavens over Ridley Park in profuse splendor, the cats' breathing synchronized, and their hearts beat in perfect unison.

Gloriana, the alert Russian Blue, broke the long silence. "It would be a cold-hearted cat who'd go home to a delicious tuna dinner and a comfortable bed this night and abandon Whiskie and his Mom to those evil men," she said quietly into the dark.

"So our part in this tragedy is to find Edeline, Buffy, and Chip, so Whiskie can comfort them. Is that what you mean?" Sunny asked.

"Yes!" Gloriana declared, nodding her bluish-grey head with unshakable faith. "That's exactly what I mean!"

Unexpectedly, Mister Backward sat straight up on his red-and-white haunches and blurted, "Buffy is my favorite human kitten!" *Kitten* is the word cats use for children.

Ordinarily Mister Backward was very bashful. Now, seeing everyone staring at him, he hastily lay back down and shyly curled his wonderfully bushy red-and-white Scottish-Fold tail over his face.

"But I've never psi-trailed before. It might take me all night to find her," Whiskie mewed. "Would any of you stay out all night with me?"

Sixteen wide little cat eyes peeked out from under the lilac bush into the dark night. The well-manicured lawn suddenly looked spooky.

"We're just poor, helpless, little show cats," Lady Practical said with a shudder. "We've never been out this late at night. We almost never even get out of our houses by ourselves. What if we get lost and can't find our way home? What if we get hurt?"

A lump of fear rose in Sunny's throat. He swallowed hard. Screwing up his courage, he declared, "I'll go."

"Me, too," BraveHeart boldly chimed in.

"A pack of wild dogs couldn't keep me home," Hildy mewed.

"I'm in," Gloriana softly purred.

One by one, they all courageously agreed to go on the journey. They were getting excited. Cats love a good adventure. Staying out all night could be fun.

Sunny sat up alertly and had a good scratch behind his golden right ear with his right hind foot--just to relax, not that he had fleas or anything. Like all his friends, he was a very clean, well-groomed show cat. He stood and stretched out his full, rounded paws. "Well, if we're going, I guess we'd better get started."

"You're such good friends!" Whiskie purred gratefully. "The black van roared away toward City Center. Let's go!"

So they set out under cover of darkness to find Whiskie's Mom and her two kittens, who were alone somewhere and in need of comfort. As he led them out from under the lilac bush, Whiskie kept to the shrubbery on the edge of the broad lawn.

With his black, bushy tail held high and the tip slightly crooked like a flag, he marched them out past Mister Backward's Tudor-style house, onto Van Buren Boulevard, and away under the street lamps. By this hour, all the Ridley Park moms were fast asleep, so no one saw Sunny and his friends disappear into the night on silent padded paws.

CHAPTER TWO

A Caged Bird Singing

Van Buren Boulevard carried the show cats in a sweeping plunge out of the Ridley Park Hills into the city below. The loud street noises from cars, trucks, and buses screeched and roared in Sunny's tender, sensitive ears. As they passed through the rackety streets, BraveHeart tried to prop up their spirits by singing. Unfortunately, he knew only one song. It went like this:

> *He was the cat with tail so dear,*
> *The cat the whole town wanted near,*
> *The cat without a single peer,*
> *The cat who brought the mail to Timaroola.*

Sunny's delicate ears soon began to hurt, and he wished the fawn-and-brown seal point Siamese would stop yowling. But BraveHeart refused to shut up. Determined to keep up his friends' courage, he sang this same verse over and over again until they came to their first alley.

Naturally, being a cat, Whiskie preferred the alley to the main thoroughfare. He made a sharp turn into the alley, and his friends dutifully followed his lead.

The damp, foul-smelling air hit Sunny's nose like a slap. A dark, narrow passageway stretched ahead of them and disappeared into the night between towering, cement-block walls beneath which grew thick patches of tall, rancid weeds. As they padded along, they passed other alleys, which ran off into the night like subterranean streams. They saw no sign of Whiskie's Mom or her kittens.

The cats traveled silently for hours in this alley world. Suddenly, Whiskie stopped short and took a turn into one of the tributary alleys. Sunny and the other show cats obediently followed. Then Whiskie took another alley, and another and another, until Sunny felt completely lost and disoriented in the dank, late-night air.

Trudging along, BraveHeart suddenly howled, "I'm hu-u-u-ungry!"

"Stop that, BraveHeart," Sunny scolded sharply. "We're not going to starve. Don't you know Whiskie's Mom will feed us when we find her? Humans always have food stashed somewhere nearby. Just keep moving. Food's no problem."

How I wish I could really believe that, Sunny thought miserably to himself. *We forgot to eat before we left home, and it's been hours since then. What I wouldn't give for a juicy piece of smoked salmon.*

The cement blocks on either side of the alley gave way to high, filthy, red-brick walls looming overhead. At ground level, they passed one dismal, locked wooden door after another. No humans, no food. How would they ever get fed?

Sunny suddenly spotted an old, rusty tomato soup can. The top was off. It looked empty. He nudged it with his nose.

"Be afraid! Be afraid!" the can cried out.

Sunny leapt back in surprise. *A talking tomato soup can? Impossible!* Scrunching down with his tail in the air, he peered deep into the can. A tiny cockroach with shiny, blue-black eyes stared shrewdly back at him. "Be afraid! Be afraid!" the cockroach squeaked excitedly. As if to emphasize the danger, the little bug danced up and down like a Mexican jumping bean.

As every cat knows, there's only one thing more important than getting fed, and that's satisfying your curiosity. Sunny ignored his rumbling tummy and cocked his golden head. "What's got you so upset?" he asked the cockroach.

Ignoring the question, the cockroach boasted, "I perform a valuable service for all who pass this way. I tell everyone, 'Be afraid! Be afraid!'"

"Of what?"

"Everything: the sky, the alley, the shadows, the dark. Be afraid! Be afraid!"

Hildy trotted up alongside Sunny and peered into the tomato soup can with him. Her tufted Norwegian Forest Cat ears were faced alertly forward and inquisitively erect. "What have you got there?" she asked.

"It's this silly cockroach," Sunny replied. "He wants us to be afraid." Addressing the cockroach, he gently coaxed, "Instead of hiding out in that filthy old can, up to your knees in slime, why don't you come out into the big, wide world and have an adventure?"

For Sunny was right: the cockroach was standing in a puddle of orange glop that looked slimy as a worm.

Sharply stung by what he perceived to be criticism of his chosen lifestyle, the cockroach stood up on his hind legs and proudly puffed out his chest. "I am a V.I.C., a Very Important Cockroach," the bug declared. "If you don't listen to me, you'll be sorry. You'll die, I tell you, you'll die. Be afraid! Be afraid!"

Suddenly, he lowered his tone and eyed Sunny suspiciously. "But I know what you want," he hissed. "You want me to leave my nice, safe can, so I'll get hurt." The cockroach firmly crossed four of his six legs across his shiny-shelled chest and defiantly turned his back on Sunny. "Well you can forget that. I'm going to stay right in here in my safe, little can and yell out a warning to everyone who passes by: You are all alone, and there is no one to save you. Be afraid! Be afraid!"

Sunny suddenly had all he could take of this irritating insect. Backing away from the can, he announced with disgust, "I'm certainly not going to let a bug tell me what to do."

"If you don't listen to me, you'll be sorry. I'm an expert. I have an I.Q. of 133. You're acting stupid. Be afraid! Be afraid!" the self-important cockroach rasped out even more loudly than before.

"C'mon, let's go," Sunny said. Hildy heartily agreed. They moved on, leaving the foolish bug alone with his warnings.

About an hour later, as he trotted alongside Hildy and BraveHeart, Sunny spied a rat perched on a pile of fetid garbage. A glaring light bulb on the wall above them cast eerie shadows over the scene. The rat sat hunched over a piece of rotten cantaloupe, gnawing off bites and gulping them hurriedly.

"Ugh!" BraveHeart shuddered with revulsion, staring at the rat. "Why on earth would any animal eat such gruesome garbage?"

"Perhaps there's no other food in this alley," Hildy replied miserably.

"Oh no! That can't be true," BraveHeart moaned. "There must be fresh cat food in here somewhere."

"Yes there is," observed Hildy, whose hunting instincts were still quite strong. "That rat is fresh cat food. But we can't catch him. None of us has ever learned how to hunt." She licked her muzzle. "We're show cats, not hunters."

Sunny lifted his golden head and looked up toward the sky. High above them, thin metal skeletons of stairsteps zig-zagged down the red-brick walls past dirty windows peering out onto the alley. The cool, damp air smelled heavy with the foul reek of crank-case drainings, diesel spills, and toxic chemicals. There was no way out.

Maybe we should be afraid, he worried to himself. *We've wound through so many alleys and turned so many corners, we have no idea how to find our way home.* A quick stab of hunger knifed through his tummy. *What if we can't get any food at all?*

On they trudged, their spirits sinking lower and lower with each weary step.

Just before dawn Mister Backward began steadily yowling, "I'm hunnn-n-n-gry!" which made them all testy. It didn't help when he wailed, "And my feeeeet hurrrrrt!"

With his red-and-white Scottish-Fold ears kinked suddenly forward and down, his rounded head, and his big, deep-blue eyes, Mister Backward looked more like an owl than a cat. Sunny's Mom, who was literary, had dubbed him the Byronic cat because everyone loved him, but if she could see and hear him now, she'd probably see him as a sad, starving character out of the *Rime of the Ancient Mariner*. When Sunny looked at the

Foldie, he could almost see his own empty stomach reflected in Backward's huge, round, blue eyes.

"When I get home tomorrow, I'm going to get a good petting," BraveHeart mewed wistfully.

Older and wiser, Lady Gloriana urged, "Cheer up, my friends. We have everything we need to get through this."

"We don't have food," the Duchess replied peevishly. "Oh, disgusting! Yuck! I just stepped into a pool of stinky, black oil. My beautiful, white, silky fur! It's ruined!"

Lady Gloriana regarded her with sympathy. "I agree things look horrible right now. But be of good cheer. We have the power of friendship. Wait and see. We'll be okay. With the power of friendship, we can do anything."

"You can't eat friendship," Duchess HighMind snapped, flipping oil off her right forepaw as she hobbled along on three legs.

Watching the Duchess gimping awkwardly down the alley, Sunny thought, *Duchess HighMind has the same problems I do. I want to see Whiskie through this mess, but it would be a disaster if I damaged my fabulous show coat!. How can I wander through these dirty, dangerous alleys at night and still keep my coat clean and bright? I've been watching out for those black puddles, and I've just missed a few myself. Maybe that's what the cockroach was warning us about. Maybe hunger is the least of our problems. Maybe I do have to 'be afraid, be afraid.' I'm the rising star in the cat shows. I've heard my Blair-Mom and Jim-Dad boast that with my rich, golden-apricot coat and muscular American Shorthair physique I'm sure to win "Best Shorthair," "Best of Breed," and "Best in Show" in my first cat show this year. How can I be Whiskie's good friend and still protect my beautiful golden coat?*

Suddenly impatient with himself, Sunny announced aloud, "Oh, stop bellyaching, you guys! Yes, we're starving and dirty and suffering, but that's okay because we're doing this for love, and love is the most important thing in the whole wide world. Love even makes the moon rise."

They plodded along silently. "How can I stop bellyaching when my belly aches so much?" the Duchess grumbled under her breath. But nobody griped quite so much after that.

Soon the alley's character shifted again, winding past tall hedges, behind which stood ramshackle houses and weedy, trash-littered yards. They had walked many long, dark miles, but had seen no trace of Whiskie's Mom and her kittens.

In some ways, that's a relief, Sunny thought to himself. *I'd be heartbroken if those wicked thieves stashed Edeline and her kittens anywhere in this depressing neighborhood.*

Her voice heavy with despair, the Duchess moaned, "The night is almost gone and we haven't found Whiskie's Mom and her two kittens. Maybe Whiskie can't psi-trail after all."

Alert to trouble, Sunny moved swiftly to place himself between the Duchess and Whiskie. He arrived just in time. The black Angora suddenly whirled angrily on the white Persian with a fierce amber glare. If Sunny hadn't come between them, Whiskie would have bitten her hard.

"If you want to quit, Duchess HighMind, go ahead! Quit! But don't lay the blame on me. Nobody asked you to come in the first place!" Whiskie snapped across Sunny's back.

"Oh, Whiskie!" the white Persian wailed to the black skies above the alleyway. "How can we find your Mom if you can't psi-trail? Do you want us to go on getting hungrier and hungrier until we just drop in our tracks?"

The disheartening idea that Whiskie did not have the gift had also crept into Sunny's mind. Starting as a vague, gnawing doubt, the fear now buzzed in his head like a swarm of angry wasps. *Could we have missed Whiskie's Mom and her kittens completely? Have we walked past them in the night? We're miles and miles from home, lost in this wretched city. If Whiskie can't psi-trail, whatever will we do?* He choked back a sob. Would they ever get petted again?

Suddenly, they heard a male cat's voice singing in a deep baritone:

> *There are cats that are loners and live by themselves*
> *Who dine all alone upon rat.*
> *I much prefer to have friends in for veal,*
> *'Cause I'm not that sort of a cat.*
> *Oh no!*
> *I'm not that sort of a cat.*
> *Ho, ho!*
> *I'm not that sort of a cat."*

They all paused, and BraveHeart peered under the hedge. "Let's have a look," he proposed. They all followed him as he quickly slipped under the hedge and emerged into a ragged, weedy backyard. Smack in the middle of the yard sat a large, shoddily-built cage made of boards and wire mesh. Staring out at them from inside the cage, his face pressed against the wire mesh, was the singer: a large bi-colored tomcat with a white body and a red head.

Sunny caught his breath at the tom's monstrous size. This cat was twice as big as any purebred Sunny had ever seen. His red-and-white coat was thick and unkempt, and his white tail was ringed with red like a raccoon's. He had a rough, ragged look that made Sunny think "moggie." (Sunny, who was working to acquire a more sophisticated vocabulary, had learned this fancy new word for a crossbreed or an alley cat, from his British shorthair friend Lady Practical.)

He so big, he has to be a moggie, Sunny thought to himself. *Purebred cats just don't get that huge.*

"Hello there, boys," said the deep-chested singer as soon as he saw Sunny and his friends standing on the edge of the lawn. "Out to have a look at the moon?"

They crossed to the cage and stared in at the prisoner.

"Why are you in that cage?" Gloriana asked.

"They got me, boys. My name's Chicago Red, and they're going to sell my carcass into the fur trade abroad. Well, maybe not my carcass. All the fur trade wants is my hide."

Suddenly, they heard one car door slam, and then a second.

"Well, they're coming back for me. So long, boys, and I wish you moon luck," Chicago Red said. "Remember me on some fine night when you're singing under the moon."

Seconds later, two cat-trappers, one short and fat and the other tall and skinny, came around the house, talking in dispirited tones. Both were mean, unpleasant men who usually had nasty adventures. But tonight, after catching the big, bi-colored tom, they'd had no further success at hurting cats, and that made them feel like failures. The short, fat man kicked open the gate, and the two men came into the backyard. Suddenly, the fat man saw the eight cats milling around the cage and froze with delight. Eight cats were a full night's work. The fat man hurriedly crossed from the gate, catching up a garden hose as he ran. Just by the way the man moved, Sunny knew they were all in for trouble.

The skinny man quickly opened the wire-mesh door so his short, fat friend could herd the cats into the cage. A wild melee followed. Two men, nine cats, and one garden hose spewing cold water got all tangled up in a wild hubbub. The ruckus ended with the fat man cursing and sucking on his bitten thumb and the skinny man whimpering and rubbing a huge red welt on his scratched forearm. Both men, now soaking wet and sorry they had ever met a cat, watched Sunny and Hildy fly around the cage in pursuit of their friends. In a second, all the cats disappeared under the hedge. The last to escape was Chicago Red. He left the cage empty.

Hunger and weariness forgotten, Sunny and his friends took to their heels like fugitives, and Chicago Red raced along with them. After they'd put a safe distance between them and that awful cage, they slowed to a trot.

Then Chicago Red did something that surprised everybody. He said, "I don't know about you, boys, but for me all this excitement has worked up quite an appetite. Is anybody here hungry?" His copper-colored eyes twinkled.

They were all struck dumb for a moment, as sudden visions of tuna, veal, and salmon danced through their heads. Finally, trying to sound dignified, Gloriana politely replied, "I can't speak for everyone here, but I could use a bite or two. Do you know where we might get a tidbit?"

"More than a tidbit — a feast!" Chicago Red laughed heartily. "And for weary travelers, a place to sleep. We'll eat 'til we drop, boys. By sunup you will all be sound asleep on full stomachs."

Prancing merrily, he led them down the alley, his red-ringed raccoon tail jauntily waving before them as they went.

CHAPTER THREE

Chicago Red's Safe House

Chicago Red led them out of the alley and through a run-down park to a long, high wooden fence. Under one broken plank of the fence, they came to a hole just large enough for one large cat to pass through. Chicago Red slipped through the hole, and the others swiftly followed.

Inside they came upon a weedy junk yard filled with old wrecked cars, piled two and three deep. "I call this my Safe House, 'cause it's the place where I'm safe," Chicago Red announced proudly. "There are more mice, chipmunks, and moles hiding in the weeds around these old broken-down cars than you can shake a tail at."

"Mice? Chipmunks? MOLES?" the Duchess replied, twitching her pink snub nose. "I thought you said you had *food*?"

"I don't see any food," whined the fawn-and-brown Siamese. "Where's the can opener, and who's going to work it?" For BraveHeart, these were honest questions.

It took Chicago Red a while to explain they had to *catch* their food. But they were all so starving they were willing to try anything. Even with hundreds of small animals of all kinds in the weeds around the piles of wrecked cars, however, the show cats very nearly went hungry.

Chicago Red at first greatly enjoyed their ineptness. He roared with laughter as mouse after chipmunk after mole got away. "Maybe you could kill your dinners by sitting on them and smothering them," he chortled. "Oh, boys, you are the funniest things I've seen in a long time."

At last Chicago Red joined in and cheerfully brought mice, moles, and chipmunks to those cats who couldn't catch their own. After a satisfying feast, they all piled into a rusty old car. As the sun peeped over the horizon and bathed the inside of the car with a rosy glow, they curled up and fell fast asleep.

* * *

Late that afternoon, toward sunset, Sunny awoke. A large, dark-grey beetle, its upper back flecked with reddish brown spots, was crawling in front of his face. The beetle slowly dragged its heavy body across the dirty, beige, plastic fabric upon which Sunny lay. Sunny squinted through one round, green eye at the beetle. *Where am I?* he thought to himself. *What am I doing here?*

Suddenly his attention snapped away from the beetle. Whiskie was jabbering excitedly. "I saw my Mom and her two kittens! I saw them!!!"

Sunny sat straight up on his golden haunches. "Where???"

The others instantly awoke. Chicago Red quickly raised his head. Lady Practical and Mister Backward bounded up onto the top of the front seat to hear the story.

"In a dream! I saw them in a dream!"

"This is a bit more like it!" Sunny exclaimed hopefully. "With the psi-trailing gift, dreams could be very important."

"They were at... a, a farm in some hills... just under some mountains. I-I-I think it's east of here. There were rivers with big waterfalls and lots and lots of Christmas trees."

Chicago Red's large, tufted ears perked up alertly. "Sounds to me, little fellow, like the foothills of The Far-Away-Mountains-to-the-East," he observed. "The tops of The Far-Away-Mountains-to-the-East are covered with forests of Christmas trees. What about them?"

"That's why we're so far from home, Chicago Red," Gloriana piped up. "Three evil men have stolen Whiskie's Mom. So Whiskie's using his psi-trailing gift to find her. That's where we're going: to find Whiskie's stolen Mom and her two kittens. Once we find them, Whiskie will stay to comfort them, and the rest of us will come home."

Chicago Red sat back on his muscular haunches and stared at the show cats with new respect. "Stolen? How monstrous! Are you going to rescue them?"

"Oh my goodness, no!" Lady Practical replied. "We're not great warriors. We're just poor, little show cats. We know about grooming and being judged. We know nothing of derring-do or dangerous rescues. But we can comfort her, and we think that's something not to be looked down on entirely."

"Oh, boys! That's noble, that is." Chicago Red's copper eyes regarded the show cats with open admiration. He turned to Whiskie. "So, all right, tell me, little fellow, were there many waterfalls in this river you saw in your dream?"

"Well, yes. One river had three waterfalls in a row, like stairs one above the other."

"I know the place," Chicago Red declared. "Spent a long, cold winter up there two years ago. That's a long way away, Whiskie. You have a great psi-trailing gift."

Something's wrong with Whiskie, Sunny worried to himself. *His voice sounds odd. This dream scares him. What's he hiding?*

"What else did you see, Whiskie?" Sunny coaxed.

"Animals. I saw animals," Whiskie said.

"What kind of animals?"

"Dogs and horses and birds. Birds bigger than me." As he spoke about the dream, Whiskie's whiskers were flattened in fear against his cheeks. Why was he so afraid?

"And?" Sunny pressed harder.

Whiskie blurted out: "The animals were all covered with blood!"

A sudden, dead silence fell inside the car. This was a dark omen indeed.

Chicago Red sprang up onto the back seat and perched on the ledge by the back window. Sunny leapt up beside him. Through the filthy, cracked window, they looked out over piles of ruined cars. Beyond the tall wooden fence surrounding Safe House loomed a high, brown hill with three white rocks halfway to the top.

"On beyond that hill," Chicago Red said, nodding through the broken window, "far, far beyond it, days and days and days, are The Far-Away-Mountains-to-the-East. The bears there are as large as small cars, boys. Wolves and coyotes and mountain lions roam there, and they're all meat-eaters."

"Then we'll get along fine," the brawny Norwegian Forest Cat chirped cheerfully. "I'm a meat-eater myself."

Chicago Red regarded Hildy thoughtfully. Such rash boldness could endanger everyone on a hazardous journey like this.

Deciding to keep his peace, he continued. "But as to where Whiskie's Mom and her kittens are, well, that I can't say. Whiskie dreamt he saw them on a farm, but those hills aren't really farming country. It's wild in those hills. I've heard there's a farm up there, but it's supposed to be deserted."

"As for that, a deserted farm might be just the place to keep something stolen," Sunny observed.

The big moggie nodded in agreement. "I can see you boys are determined to go on."

"If your mom needed comfort, wouldn't you go?" Sunny asked.

"I surely would. But what you're proposing involves much more than just finding and comforting Whiskie's Mom. The weather will be changing soon. Winter may come on before you can reach those mountains."

"No one ever said a cat should comfort its Mom only if she's in a nice, safe, warm place," Lady Practical observed. "I for one can only go east toward those hills because that's where my friend Whiskie has to go."

"Why can't Chicago Red go with us?" BraveHeart asked.

"No," Sunny replied. "He's already done more than we have a right to ask by rescuing us from the alleys and letting us stay here in his Safe House."

"But I can teach you to hunt before you go," Chicago Red chirruped brightly. "By the time I'm done with you, with all the mice and chipmunks you'll catch to eat, you'll just get fat on your journey."

So for three more nights, the show cats lingered in Chicago Red's Safe House, and the big moggie taught them to hunt. With the instincts inherited from her Viking ancestors, Hildy caught on quickly. Mister Backward, surprisingly, turned out to be the best hunter. But he never lorded it over anyone, and they all appreciated that.

At sunset on the fifth night, as they prepared to leave, Chicago Red leaped into the old, rusty car and landed lightly beside Sunny. "I've changed my mind. I want to go with you."

"What?" Sunny gulped with surprise.

"Look, you guys are no good in the wild. None of you will last until you get to those hills. You need a savvy cat like me. And I still owe you."

Sunny gasped so hard in astonishment he almost swallowed his tongue. The other cats pricked up their ears. Whiskie whirled and stared at the big, bi-colored tom with amazed, amber eyes.

"What's that? What did you say?" Whiskie demanded.

Puzzled, Chicago Red replied, "I said, I want to go with you."

"No. After that. You said, 'You need a savvy cat like me. And I still owe you.'"

"Yeah. Well, I am, little fellow. And you do," Chicago Red replied.

Whiskie turned to Sunny. "Don't you remember? That's what the fire cat said in my dream vision. And fire is red and white. Sunny, we just have to take Chicago Red with us. He's the fire cat."

Being polite, as most cats are, Chicago Red went off by himself to give them a chance to talk freely. The Duchess and Mister Backward were opposed to the idea of taking him along. Chicago Red seemed open and friendly enough. But he was also strange, wild, and uncivilized. He called them all "boys," when Lady Practical, Hildy, Lady Gloriana, and the Duchess were plainly fine ladies. Should they risk accepting this rough, unkempt moggie into their pampered, dignified circle? If he ever showed up at a cat show with his unsightly, bedraggled coat, the judges would laugh him right off the stage. What if he tried to take charge and run everything? He seemed to want to be their guide, but Whiskie was already their guide. Whiskie had the gift. Could this huge moggie really be trusted? Despite all this, Lady Practical strongly favored letting him come. Her reasons, of course, were mostly practical. He could teach them how to live in the wild, and he knew exactly where the foothills were. Whiskie, of course, insisted Chicago Red just *had* to come along because he was the fire cat in the dream.

Sunny finally settled the matter by pointing out Chicago Red had said he still owed them. None of them believed that, of course, because he'd already done so much by teaching them to hunt. But he was acting as a true friend, and they all felt they should respond as good friends and take him along. With that said, even Duchess HighMind and Mister Backward reversed their opinions. They were all firm believers in friendship.

"All right, boys! You won't regret this," the big moggie exclaimed when Sunny told him they would be deeply honored if he would come with them. The moggie added, "But as names are very important to cats, before we leave I'm going to give the bunch of you a name. You're the most special clowder of cats I've ever met, so I'm going to give you a special name. From now on, you will be known as 'The Friendship.'"

"Why that's excellent," agreed the Duchess. "We are going to aid Whiskie's Mom and her two kittens, and in bygone times, 'friendship' used to mean 'aid, help or assistance.'"

The others did not care about old obscure meanings of words. They did, however, like friendship and would enjoy belonging to one.

"Yes," Sunny said, "I like that. That's what we are: The Friendship." With that, The Friendship and Chicago Red set out in high spirits to find Whiskie's Mom and her two kittens, who were somewhere in the foothills of The Far-Away-Mountains-to-the-East, alone and in need of comforting.

As he followed Mister Backward's red tail under the fence and out of Safe House, Sunny wondered if they should have laid down rules for Chicago Red. But, no, how could they make him obey them, anyway? Besides, Sunny's mind was preoccupied with much more pressing worries. Why, at the farm where Whiskie's Mom and her kittens were being held prisoners, were the animals all covered with blood?

CHAPTER FOUR

Hard Going in the Rain

The Friendship was clearly a different bunch than the show cats who'd capered down Van Buren Boulevard a few nights earlier. They had grown raggle-taggle. The long-haired Duchess had knots, tangles, and mats in her once-silky coat. Sunny's always impeccably clean golden paws were now smudged with dirt. Still, for the first time in their lives, they forgot to care about how they looked. They each knew that in the darkest hour, when all appeared lost, they had stuck together and learned to catch dinner.

In the cool air of sunset, the cats raced past the three white rocks to the top of the brown hill. They stood up to their ribs in short, dry grass, panting pleasantly. Sunny gazed toward the horizon at the rolling hills, distant, purple, and menacing. "Are those hills as steep as this one?" he asked.

"Some are steeper," Chicago Red replied grimly. "For the first part of our journey, we'll have it rough. The hills grow steep and steeper. Once we come out into the Great Valley, the traveling gets easy. We'll pass through flat country filled with farms and all kinds of tasty, little animals, fattened up on grain. The valley is miles across. Then come the foothills."

"And what happens there?" Mister Backward asked.

"If Whiskie is right, those are the hills where his Mom's being held, and our journey again will get really tough. There are huge hills, great roaring rivers, and very few paths. The hunting is also poor, no chipmunks and few mice.

Unwilling to linger long over the dangers ahead, impulsive, young BraveHeart shouted, "Let's get started!"

And off they ran, charging down the eastern slope of the brown hill, across the narrow valley, and up the next hill, heading east, ever east.

Lady Practical, who was seven-years-old, soon grew testy about BraveHeart pushing them so hard.

But BraveHeart wouldn't let up. "I know you're getting old, Lady Practical," he teased with a twinkle in his sapphire-blue eyes. "But you have to keep up with everyone else. No special deals for the elderly."

"I'll show you something, you young show-off. I'll show you my tail!" Practical snapped indignantly.

As she charged ahead into the lead, BraveHeart instantly took up the challenge and raced after her. The other cats, caught up in the competition, began to cheer.

"Way to go, Lady Practical!" Gloriana shouted. "British Shorthairs beat Siamese every time."

"BraveHeart, you stop chasing that old cat right now!" cried another.

Although Lady Practical held the lead for a short while, BraveHeart soon caught and passed her. Poor Practical had to accept the others' views of her: at seven, she was old for a cat, middle-aged.

BraveHeart happily frolicked along. Holding him back was about as easy as holding back the winter wind with a screen door.

Late that night, as the cats trotted along the crest of a hogback, the rain began. The hogback plunged steeply down on both sides into tree-filled valleys. The ridge was so high it was as if they had found a pathway among the clouds.

Will we be safe up here on this ridge in a strong wind and driving rain? Sunny worried to himself. *What if one of us gets blown off the trail?* He peered down the steeply plunging slopes on both sides of the ridge and shuddered at the sight of the long drop below. Then he reminded himself: *It's late. You're tired. Try not to think about it.* He carefully placed one paw in front of the other, praying as he went that he wouldn't stumble and fall. With most of his reserves exhausted, weariness settled on him like a cloak of clay.

Through the rest of the night, BraveHeart browbeat them to keep moving. From the head of the line, the energetic Siamese shouted, "Come on. How can you move at this snail's pace? You're breaking Whiskie's heart when you drag along."

Finally, exhausted and almost asleep on their feet, they came down off the hogback into a wildflower meadow, where they gratefully met the dawn. A heavy mist hung thick over the meadow. As the sun rose, its light struck the mist and the meadow shimmered like a lake of fiery gold. In the shelter of a Mexican elderberry, they all cuddled together in a tangled pile of cat fur that kept everyone toasty warm. In the cat pile, Duchess HighMind's snow-white chin lay across Mister Backward's creamy-white back. Backward's chin rested on Gloriana's greyish-blue ribs. Gloriana's paw rested atop Chicago Red's red-and-white head, and so on and so forth. You have to be good cat friends to sleep like this. But, if you can, it's wonderfully warm and chummy.

They awoke at sunset to agony and stiffness. Once they realized they were sore all over because BraveHeart had pushed them so hard the night before, a general peevishness set in toward the seal point Siamese. When they got on the trail again and BraveHeart began moaning about his sore leg muscles, no one felt the least sympathy for him.

Shortly before midnight, when they had at last worked out some of the soreness, the rain opened up and poured down in torrents. They quickly became a soaked and sorry-looking bunch of bedraggled cats. During the worst of the storm, they were caught between two hills in a broad valley that contained not a rock nor a bush for shelter. By the time they found protection under a massive sycamore on the far edge of the valley, they were drenched, scraggly, and muddy.

"My poor coat! My poor coat! It will never be the same again," the Duchess moaned.

BraveHeart had no patience with her vanity. "What's the use, Duchess?" he said. "We can't stay clean out here. Let it go."

Her determination up, the Persian replied, "The important thing is making an effort, BraveHeart. Trying keep a handsome coat builds character."

BraveHeart and Mister Backward were shivering miserably. Whiskie looked especially pitiful, which greatly worried Sunny. In Ridley Park, his black friend had always been friendly and playful. But since shouldering the burden of psi-trailing, he had become thin and drawn. He now had a fragile air about him and a far-away look in his amber eyes, as if he were watching a mystery shrouded in fog.

At Sunny's urging, the cats rearranged themselves, with BraveHeart, Backward, and Whiskie in the middle. The others huddled close around them to share their warmth.

"We want to get to Whiskie's Mom as quickly as possible and then back to our own homes, but we're not going one step farther until you three are all right," Sunny told them. Sunny's idea worked brilliantly. Soon they were all warm again, and Whiskie's eyes began to look slightly more focused.

"Okay, let's go," Sunny announced.

"I don't know, Sunny," Duchess said, stopping him. "Maybe we should stay right here and rest. We're all warm, and I've seen signs of field mice."

Sunny smiled. *A week ago*, he thought, *a field mouse could have run over her tail and not gotten her attention. Now signs of field mice are signs of dinner, and she hasn't missed them.* He turned his head to speak to the Persian, and his jaw flew open. There, before his eyes, sat a bright, glowing, almost snow-white Duchess HighMind.

"Duchess, you look absolutely splendid!" Sunny exclaimed, very impressed.

"Why thank you, Sunny." she replied with a purr. "I feel so much better now. I just removed a few mats and burrs. Burrs are such a problem in a fine coat like mine. How about it, Sunny? Should we stop here for the day?"

Sunny slowly shook his head. "I understand how you feel, and I'm tired, too, Duchess. But what if those mean men hurt Whiskie's Mom? I'll bet she's scared, and really needs Whiskie's comfort. We have to get to her as fast as possible."

Being warm and dry had felt good. But once they set out again, they were soon drenched. Toward dawn, they found shelter for the day's sleep under a tall, leaning rock which kept off the chill storm wind. Under the rock, the Duchess patiently showed Gloriana some of her tricks for keeping her coat silky, burrless, and free of dirt. Afterwards Gloriana looked magnificent, and everyone demanded the Persian's help. The Duchess promised to help them all in the days ahead, for as everyone knows, making the effort to keep a clean coat builds character.

Unfortunately, the following night was even more miserable, and the Duchess's tricks helped no one. It poured almost nonstop. Two days and nights of rain had driven the little animals underground, so hunting was bad. The cats went hungry the entire night.

Finally, just before sunrise, like an unexpected crescendo in a piece of music, the sky cleared. The day dawned bright and shining with a promise of sun and comforting warmth. Just before they stopped for the day, they stumbled onto a city of field mice and had a magnificent feast.

As the sun climbed over the horizon to the east, they found a cozy spot to bed down under a patch of castor bean plants. The broad, pointed-lobe leaves covered them like little umbrellas, which would be handy if the rain started up again. All around grew sweet fennel, and its licorice smell filled the air.

"It's been a good night," purred the well-fed Practical with satisfaction, as she turned around several times, finding the best position to sleep for the day.

"How on earth could you call what we just went through a good night?" demanded the Duchess. She lay down behind Practical and propped her neck and chin across her brown tabby friend's back. Soon all the cats were in a helter-skelter, willy-nilly, chummy pile.

"It ended with a good dinner, didn't it?" Practical replied.

As he dozed off with Whiskie's black chin and forepaws lying across his golden ears, Sunny took Lady Practical's reply as a sign they were adjusting to the wild. They now considered ending the night with a decent dinner a sign the whole night had been good. What more could a little cat want?

CHAPTER FIVE

Of *Meena-Oomas* and Name Keepers

The day remained bright and cheery with fair blue skies. When they awoke that afternoon just before sunset, however, ominous grey clouds began to gather over the hills. As they set out on the trail, the drenching rain began again. Even when the rain stopped, the clouds settled in and hung low overhead, black and threatening. Sharp, chill winds whistled through the hills and cut through their fur coats, making them shiver as they padded along a high, majestic ridge.

Sunny was bringing up the rear alone. Up high, even on this dark and cloudy night, he could see for long distances – almost as well as you and I can see in bright sunlight. That's because at the back of each of his eyes, Sunny had a wondrous little mirror – called a *tapetum lucidum*. This glittering layer of bright cells reflected back any light that passed through his retina, which improved his night vision and made his eyes glow in the dark. Unfortunately, even with his extra-sharp eyesight, the golden American Shorthair saw no end of the brooding black hills rolling before them in the distance. *Will we ever reach the Great Valley?* he wondered. *Chicago Red said we'll eventually come to it. He said the journey will get easier once we reach the Great Valley and we come out on its flat, level table-top. Oh, how I wish we'd get there soon!* As they trudged wearily over one steep hill after another, the hope of easier traveling ahead buoyed his spirits.

As they came down one hill and crossed a wide clearing, Hildy dropped back beside him, and Sunny sensed she wanted to talk.

They traveled along in silence. Then Hildy said, "This third name business bothers me, Sunny. I've got a name for the show and a name for around the house. How many names do I need to have?"

Sunny understood. *Names are a bother,* he thought to himself. *They bother me and all my friends. Tradition has it that every cat is supposed to have three names. My first, official name is "Heartland's Sun at the Morning of Manning." "Heartland's" is the cattery where I was born. "Sun at the Morning" is a bit my Mom added because she likes it. And "Manning," my Mom's last name, tells people I'll be available to father purebred American Shorthair kittens. All that is just my first name. My second, short, everyday name is "Sunny." But now I'm supposed to have yet a third, secret name that I choose for myself. What a ridiculous mess!*

Speaking aloud, he told Hildy, "The old cats say two names aren't enough."

"I know. And I suppose I must find another one. Do you have your third name yet?"

He wanted to say, "Champion." He knew his Mom and Dad wanted him to be one.

"Yes, Hildy, I have a third name. But the old cats say you're supposed to pronounce your secret name only once, and that's to your Name Keeper." It was understood between him and Whiskie that they would be each other's Name Keepers. He was Whiskie's Name Keeper, and he knew Whiskie's secret name was "DreamSpinner."

"I know. 'One time counts for all time.' I've heard that old saying many times."

"You know, I think there are many mysteries about secret names we're never told," Sunny continued. "It seems to me you have to *mean* your secret name. If you don't, that's like not saying it at all."

Hildy gave him a puzzled look. "I don't understand."

"Well, we're told a secret name is for our *Meena-Oomas*. But no cat ever tells us what our *Meena-Oomas* really are. Some of the older cats even talk as if *Meena-Oomas* are something inside us more real than our claws and teeth. But I don't think they mean that."

"No," agreed the Weegie, who was rapidly becoming a fine hunter. "Not more real than our claws and teeth."

"I think, even though none of the older cats have ever said this, that our *Meena-Oomas* are our ambitions. The way I figure it, the *Meena-Ooma* defines our dreams. That's why we don't name our *Meena-Oomas* until we're old enough to have an ambition."

Hildy sighed deeply.

"I wish I could see things as clearly you do, Sunny. I don't understand anything you've said. I have no ambitions at all, so I guess I shouldn't even take a third name. But it's part of being a cat, so I guess I will."

"That's okay," Sunny replied. "I don't understand it, either."

Just then Chicago Red dropped back to walk along beside them. The tip end of his bushy tail was twitching in agitation. *What's he so worked up about?* Sunny wondered to himself. *He's usually so calm.*

"Do you boys always cross clearings strung out like this?" the big moggie asked. "You're turning me into a nervous wreck. I've been watching you guys court disaster since we started across this clearing."

"Why? What's wrong?" Sunny asked.

"Why don't you just ask, What's wrong with getting eaten?" Chicago Red snorted.

"There's no danger in sight. Where's the boogie rat?" Sunny retorted, his voice rising.

The others overheard the disagreement and moved closer to defend Sunny.

"Here it comes," the Duchess whispered under her breath to Practical. "I warned you we'd have trouble with this rough moggie."

"Owls!" Chicago Red announced, spitting out the word as if it were a stink bug he'd accidentally bitten. He continued walking at his own steady pace, but not without noting that he had suddenly become surrounded by the Duchess, Practical, and Gloriana. He thought to himself, *This is a rare bunch of cats. They certainly do look out for each other.*

Then he said aloud, without missing a beat, "Owls just love to dine on cat. I've seen the evidence under their trees."

"What evidence?" Gloriana demanded.

"Owl pellets, boys. An owl eats whatever he catches entire. But he can't digest it entire. So he eats grass, leaves, and twigs, and then he coughs up the undigested bits of his dinner, all wrapped up in a neat little pellet. Several times in my life, I've found owl pellets under trees, and more than once I discovered the undigested parts were cat skulls."

"So what?" Hildy asked. "We'd hear any bird big enough to be dangerous long before he could catch us."

"Not an owl," Chicago Red corrected her. "Owls dive swiftly and silently, and their claws can break your back with one blow. The rest of us might not even hear you cry out. When we reached the other side of the clearing, we'd only say, 'Where's Hildy?' But no one would know."

Hildy laughed as if he'd just told a good joke. She was a big, physical cat who had never been afraid in her life. The threat of an owl wasn't about to scare her.

"Then I would be a mystery. And you'd never forget me," she chuckled.

"Owls don't scare you?"

"An owl's just a big bird, Chicago Red. I eat birds."

Chicago Red let it go. *Why be an alarmist?* he thought sourly to himself. *There'll be time to show her she should be afraid. If she lives that long.*

Silently, they plodded on into the night.

CHAPTER SIX

A Message from the Moon

It was their fifth night in the wild fields before they saw the moon. The rain had stopped, and the cats had made a long, tiring pull up a steep hill wooded with stately oak trees and populated by crickets sawing in the night and owls hooting in the distance. The woods were alive with dusky shadows and mysterious smells. As the cats approached, rabbits playing under the oaks scattered before them and scampered away into the shadows.

They trudged up the steep path through a wet, thick layer of last year's leaves. Silently, a wolfish beast with a long, bushy tail picked them up, shadowed them over the crest, and coasted easily alongside them down toward a flat field that stretched away on the valley floor.

Spying the beast in the shadows, Mister Backward asked, "Is that a wild animal, Chicago Red?" The Foldie was barely able to contain his excitement.

"About as wild as they come, little fellow. That's a coyote. A coyote won't bother you if he's not hungry. But an old feral cat saying goes 'Beware the coyote with hungry feet.' See how he keeps his feet moving all the time? If a dog kills a deer, he'll play with it or carry off some of it. A hungry coyote will pick the bones clean."

"That's one hungry-footed coyote," Sunny said uneasily. The coyote's feet gave him the creeps. They required no effort to feint easy, graceful lunges at the clowder of cats. Chicago Red and The Friendship stopped and bunched close together. They stood up to their knees in last year's leaves, which turned to wet mush under their shifting feet. The larger cats surrounded Whiskie, who mewed in terror and looked suddenly pitiful and small.

Eying Whiskie, the coyote crooned, "What's that you've got there, my sweet little darlings? A nice, little, black, tasty morsel? Why don't you let me have him – just the little black one – and I'll let the rest of you go free." Saliva dripped from his long yellow fangs.

The cats huddled more tightly together as the coyote stalked closer. His feet did an evil dance in the low grass. "You want to be free? Give him to me!" he repeated in an oily voice. A horse fly buzzed around his right ear, and the coyote snapped violently at it with his strong, heavy jaws. He moved closer until his nose was only inches from the clowder.

Suddenly, Chicago Red made a wide, rapid swipe with his razor-sharp claws and scratched hard, leaving four deep welts across the coyote's tender black nose.

The coyote yelped and drew back in pain. "Why did you do that? I was just kidding. You didn't have to do that. That was mean," the big bully whimpered, patting delicately at his scratched nose with his left front paw. Then his voice shifted again. "Oh, it's all right," he said silkily. "I forgive you. Come here. Let's hug and make up."

Refusing to be deceived, Chicago Red hissed, "Before you get Whiskie, you'll have to fight us all."

The coyote glared and slunk further back, just far enough for the cats to move quickly on down the steep path under the oaks. The big bully continued to follow them at a distance, which unnerved everyone. Finally, as they passed out of the woods and came onto the valley floor, the coyote dropped back and disappeared. Everyone breathed a deep sigh of relief.

As they padded along the valley floor in the close darkness BraveHeart asked plaintively, "Do any of you miss your moms the way I do?"

"I miss my Mom's warmth, perfume, and soft voice," Gloriana said with a deep longing in her voice.

"You know what I miss the most?" asked the Duchess. "The petting. I used to sit on my Mom's lap for hours. She would pet me and pet me and pet me."

"Ah, yes. A good scratch behind the ears. That's what I need," mused Practical. "It was pure bliss, wasn't it?"

Sticking closer together than ever, Sunny and his friends reached a meadow in the valley. They trotted through the meadow along the edge of a broad, flat field, where the grass had been closely cut and made into square little bundles. On their left grew a fencerow of Jerusalem artichokes, wild buckwheat, and giant coreopsis. On their right, the field dotted with the bundles of cut grass was shining brighter and brighter. A silver luminosity lay over the land.

Sunny thought the field seemed too well-lighted for this late after sunset. And then he saw it. Rising above the tree tops to the east of the meadow was a large, round, luminous globe that seemed to have been placed in the sky as a signal to him. Though the globe seemed large, the light was gentle and soft yet powerful enough that Sunny knew this was why the field seemed unusually lighted.

"What is *that*?" Sunny asked, amazed and bewildered.

"Why, that's the moon," answered Duchess HighMind. Sunny and Whiskie gazed directly at the lovely golden-white globe. The white Persian watched with detached amusement as her two young friends gaped with awed perplexity at it. "Hasn't either of you seen the moon before?"

"Not like that," Whiskie whispered.

I agree, Sunny thought to himself. *The moon never looked this breathtaking through a window. Other cats who've been outside at night told me, "I don't know why; but the moon in the window is not the same as the moon in the sky." Now I see they were right.* Hanging low in the huge hollow sky, surrounded by thousands of stars, this unique moon shone with a soft, sweet radiance so full of power Sunny could not look at anything else. From horizon to horizon, the glowing sphere dominated the sky with a dazzling, magical light that was not at all like the smiling, benign mother who had always stared back at him in its case of window. This most-certainly-different moon sent a soothing message of friendship that made him think of hope, peace, and courage. He was totally unprepared for its grandeur and beauty. Compared to the sky, it was just a small globe of light, but its presence was huge, striking, and bold.

Unable to tear his gaze from the spectacular light, Sunny gulped his astonishment. His round eyes, huge and wide, glowed like gold-green fire in the moonlight. "Oh, my gosh!"

"We cats have a deep, abiding love for the moon," said the Duchess. "That's one reason we do not believe the night was made for evil. It's a wonderful time to feel on intimate terms with the most far-flung stars. The Night Mother fascinates us as humans are fascinated by great art. We sing songs to the moon, call her 'Queen of the Night' or 'Night Mother,' tell stories about her, and wish each other 'moon luck.' We can sit for hours looking at her in the sky or at her reflection in water. We are born with a love for Night Mother, which never leaves our hearts."

"But that can't be the moon," Whiskie protested.

Duchess HighMind looked surprised. "And why not?"

"Because it's a light someone put there as a signal to me," he calmly explained.

The Duchess chuckled to herself. "Many cats think the moon is his or her personal message. But from whom the message comes we've never been able to determine. Some say it's just a big rock in the sky."

"That's ridiculous. It's obviously a message."

"Why not a big rock?"

"Duchess HighMind," Whiskie retorted with disapproval, "I don't have to explain to a cat with your mental powers that if it were a rock it would fall out of the sky."

The white Persian with the high regal forehead now blazing in the moonlight had no concept of the workings of gravity. Nor did she know how a satellite stays in place by centripetal force. But she was wise enough to know there were many things on earth and in heaven she did not understand. "You could be right, Captain White Whiskers," she replied softly. "I, too, have felt the message call me by name."

All the cats sat silently side by side, breathing in unison, struck in wonder at the moon.

Chicago Red at last broke the long silence. "Come on, boys," he said gently, "we should be getting on."

Without a murmur, they all followed after him, setting off along the fencerow in the warm, mystical light.

More than once that night, both Whiskie and Sunny tripped and stumbled as they gazed up at the great globe of light. About dawn, Chicago Red found a dry stream bed that led them like a wide highway toward the mountains.

Yet even then Sunny could not take his eyes off Night Mother. "With a moon like this in my memory," the golden American Shorthair silently vowed, "I'll never again ask, What difference can one little cat make?" For the rest of the night, he moved at a faster pace with a lighter step. "Night Mother! I've seen Night Mother in person!" And once more the freshness of the land and the goodness of its freedom came back to him.

CHAPTER SEVEN

Clouds of Death! Clouds of Death!

One night when the moon had shrunk to half-round, the cats came into a land rough and wild. They followed a dry stream bed as it cut its way through a thick, dark, oak forest sprinkled with hickory and elm. At times in the distance through the trees, Sunny glimpsed high, rugged cliffs, deep canyons, and plunging waterfalls. This was not a land for softies, but that was okay. They were no longer pampered show cats.

The first day in the wild land, they slept in the shelter of a thick stand of mule fat, which grew abundantly on the banks of the dry stream bed. That evening, after hunting and feeding themselves, the cats continued to follow the dry creek bed as a trail. Night came on, and the predators awakened. Coyotes howled in the distance. A bobcat screamed, which made all their hackles stand on end.

The next night, the stream bed narrowed and turned directly north. Following Whiskie's lead, they abandoned the dry creek bed and struck off at an angle through a deep oak forest. Heading east, they soon put the hostile land behind them.

Shortly before dawn, they came into a region where trees produced all kinds of fruit: oranges, grapefruit, peaches, limes, plums, and lemons. They slept by day in the groves, always traveling by night. Unfortunately, the fruit groves produced few small prey or insects. Having almost nothing to hunt, they frequently went hungry.

One day, fresh after sunrise, they came into a grove where there was absolutely nothing to hunt. Disappointed but determined to make the best of a bad situation, they went to sleep on nine empty, growling tummies.

About mid-morning, everyone woke up with a start. Whiskie was crying in a pitiful voice that filled them with fear.

"Clouds of death! Clouds of death!" he moaned. He ran wildly about and clawed at his friends, trying to drive them out from under the trees.

Caught up by the fear in Whiskie's voice, the other cats all retreated from him. No one knew what to make of his strange behavior. They gave into a kind of panic and began to flee from the mad Turkish Angora, crying in misery.

Then Sunny caught another noise. It started as a weak droning sound. But it grew quickly in volume until it was a powerful roar and then a loud thunder that drowned out Whiskie's cries of despair. Looking up between two trees, Sunny saw a great bird flying overhead. It roared violently, injecting its noise into the tranquil peace of the grove. Immediately Sunny saw it was not a great bird, but a great machine.

"Run for it, boys!" Chicago Red suddenly screamed. "Run like you've never run before!"

They fled the fruit-tree grove and escaped into a field of high grass and weeds. As they looked back, white smoke billowed out from beneath the machine. The grove they had just left behind vanished in a white cloud.

"What's that, Whiskie?" Sunny asked. "Do you know?"

Whiskie shook his head. His voice trembled. "I just saw in my dream that machine flying over the field, letting out that cloud, except it was black with death."

"You saved our lives," Chicago Red declared.

"How did he save our lives? What was that?" asked the Duchess.

"It's a flying machine men use to put that cloud on fields and fruit trees. It kills things. That's why we couldn't find any mice or bugs to hunt under those trees. If Whiskie had not heard the flying machine ahead of time, that cloud would have caught us under those trees, and we'd be dead, too. It's a good thing you were sleeping lightly," Chicago Red added.

"I was sleeping soundly, dreaming, and I didn't hear the machine," Whiskie corrected him. "I heard it for the first time just before it flew over our heads."

The Duchess said, "What he's saying is undoubtedly true, Chicago Red. Whiskie has very powerful — and very strange — dreams."

"There's no doubt about it," Sunny agreed. "Whiskie's mystical powers are growing."

"Could be. He's among friends," Gloriana chimed in. "Whatever our talents, we do them better among friends. That's the way with friendship: it always strengthens what's best in us."

Sunny did not argue with her. It occurred to him Gloriana was onto something with her "power-of-friendship" idea, but he wasn't sure what.

CHAPTER EIGHT

A Secret from the Past

Then one night, a few days after leaving the fruit groves behind, they were following a stream along a valley that cut deep between two hills. Abruptly, they emerged onto the edge of a broad, flat land stretching away as far as the eyes could see.

"What's this?" Sunny asked happily. No more hills! The realization hit him with joy.

"This is it, boys: the Great Valley," Chicago Red answered. "We're now about a third of the way to the foothills. From here on, the traveling will be easier and the food less work."

"I thought a valley would dip down. This is so flat!" exclaimed Mister Backward.

"We've been dipping down for hours," Chicago Red replied. "You just never noticed it."

As they trotted along, Sunny thought to himself, *For all our dependence on Chicago Red and his advice, none of us has fully accepted him. Our pasts come between us and keep us from becoming dear friends. We're show cats, after all, and he's just a moggie. He's a little too coarse, a little too rough. None of us has reached that easy-going way with him that makes a relationship move smoothly over to friendship before either party has thought much about it.*

For his part, Chicago Red knew full well he was not accepted by The Friendship. But he stayed good-humored about it. He had adopted a friendly but aloof attitude toward them, as if they were children he regarded with amused tolerance.

One night, as the cats marched along under the star-flecked sky, relishing the easy travel though the Great Valley, Chicago Red said, "You know, boys, I admire what you're doing. You're okay. Not like most show cats I've met."

"What are you talking about?" Hildy demanded irritably. "Show cats are the finest examples of cats. We are especially clean and constantly try to be more perfect. By trying to be better cats, we gain deeper spiritual insights into life. Why, I'll bet a moggie like you doesn't even have a third name."

"Hildy!" Practical exclaimed. "What a rude thing to say. He may be a moggie, but he has a *Meena-Ooma*, and we should respect it."

Chicago Red shook his head. "No, no, it's all right. Don't scold her. She's correct. I don't have three names. Never did, never will. I'm Chicago Red and Chicago Red is me."

"You're right, Lady Practical. It was rude. And I apologize to you, Chicago Red." As if trying to make up for her blunder, Hildy added, "And I even envy you a little. Secret names are such a bother. I may just forget about mine."

But Chicago Red protested, "Oh you can't do that, Hildy. Choosing a secret name is one of the most difficult but critical decisions a young cat will ever make. It is important beyond everything. I made my first trip into the wilds to find mine."

Sunny looked surprised. "I thought you said you didn't have a third name?"

"I don't have a *third* name. But that's because I don't have a name like 'Kutie Kitty Korner's Fluffy Face of Big Breeder.' If you want to call me to dinner, you can only call me Chicago Red. But that doesn't mean I don't have a secret name for my *Meena-Ooma*. I named my *Meena-Ooma* a long time ago."

Sunny felt relieved. He was glad to hear Chicago Red had a secret name, although he wasn't sure why.

"Well there you go, Hildy," Sunny said. "Here's someone you can talk to about choosing your name. I'm sure he'll agree with me that when picking a name you need to think about your ambitions."

"Ambitions?" Chicago Red hooted. "Is that where you're choosing yours, Sunny?"

"What makes you so certain I'm still choosing mine?" Sunny replied defensively. "Why couldn't I have already picked it?"

Ignoring the question, Chicago Red spoke to the whole group: "Boys, the *Meena-Ooma's* buried deep inside you, so deep it's hard to find. It is a critical part of you, even more important than one of your vital organs like your heart or your lungs. But just as your heart can make you sick when something's wrong with it, when something is wrong with your *Meena-Ooma*, it shows up in your behavior. And that's why they say, 'The happy cat has found its *Meena-Ooma*. The subtle cat has named its *Meena-Ooma*. But the fearless cat has become its *Meena-Ooma*.'"

"What makes you think I haven't named my *Meena-Ooma*?" Sunny demanded irritably.

"Because you haven't found your *Meena-Ooma* yet," Chicago Red matter-of-factly replied. "And I suspect you are not even looking in the right place. Tell me something about these names you're thinking of choosing. Not the names themselves, of course. But tell me a little about them."

"I'm thinking about a name that has to do with my show business ambitions," Sunny said proudly.

Chicago Red looked disappointed.

"Something wrong with that?"

"For a dainty little feline with a satin cushion, I guess that's OK. But you're no such animal. Think about a name that has to do with the quality of your *Meena-Ooma*."

"But my *Meena-Ooma's* qualities have to do with show business."

Chicago Red said, "I don't care if you had your fur all fluffed up with talcum powder and your tail tied in red ribbons. Your *Meena-Ooma* is like mine. It's wild and free but also loving."

Sunny protested, "There you go. You're doing it, too."

"Doing what?"

"Talking like the old cats. Talking as if the *Meena-Ooma* is another cat inside each of us, but more real than our teeth and claws."

"And what on earth do you believe it is *except* that?"

"For different cats, it's different things. But for me it's just my ambitions."

"Now there *you* go, talking like every foolish young cat with half a brain in his head. And I suppose you think that for another cat, the *Meena-Ooma* might be a talent for singing or for telling stories?"

"Yes. It might be that." Sunny replied. Then, suddenly, his curiosity overcame his pride. "Exactly what do you think it is?"

They passed into a wood and trotted along in the deep, dark shadows under the trees. Bright stars peeped occasionally between the thick leaves overhead. Chicago Red turned his head to study Sunny.

"A cat's secret name is given to that part of himself he most wishes to strengthen, the *Meena-Ooma*. But the *Meena-Ooma* is deep and private. It's not to be talked about. We say the name of our *Meena-Ooma* to our Name Keeper, so the name will be real. But we never again speak it aloud. In this way, we gain a powerful self-awareness and spiritual strength unavailable to those who do not have secret names. When in danger, or when being put to an important test, a cat may be heard to say, 'I will call upon my secret name.' And this secret name, the name of his strength, will save him. He never allows anyone to make fun of his secret name, nor to treat it lightly. The secret name gives him character and fortifies him against all kinds of failures."

Sunny said restlessly, "You make choosing a secret name sound like a high art. That if a cat is not careful, he can make a serious mistake in naming his *Meena-Ooma*."

"Then you've been listening carefully because that's exactly what I mean. That's why your secret name is so important. It's what makes you different from all other animals in creation. Sometimes you'll meet a cat who's cowardly or just not doing well, and one day you'll hear that cat say, 'It is my fault. I named my *Meena-Ooma* poorly.'"

"Well, where is this *Meena-Ooma*? In what part of a cat is it located?"

Chicago Red looked steadily at Sunny. "Like most special, unique things, the *Meena-Ooma* is hard to find. And even once you've found it, it can be hard to remember. That's why we name our *Meena-Oomas*. So we won't forget them, so we can become them. For instance, I named mine right after an event that made me keenly aware of my *Meena-Ooma*. I tell you, boys, around the campfires in the hills under The-Far-Away-Mountains-to-the-East, they're still telling the story of what happened that night. Not wanting to forget what happened, I named my *Meena-Ooma* on the spot."

"Of course, you cannot tell us."

"Oh, I can tell you the circumstances. But, as you know, I can't tell you the name."

"Well, then, what were the circumstances?"

"It happened two winters ago, up in those hills where we're going." And here he paused to bound over a large root of a huge sycamore tree. The others followed him as he continued, "It happened while I was escaping from three men and a pack of hunting dogs."

Lady Practical regarded him with a mixture of curiosity and disbelief. "You and another cat were being chased by three men and a pack of hunting dogs?"

"No," Chicago Red said. "There was no other cat present."

"Then who was your Name Keeper?"

"You have to remember this: a Name Keeper only has to be a friend you know and respect, someone who knows and respects you. My Name Keeper is not a cat."

They were all so amazed at this, they came to a complete stop in a deep shadow under a wide-branched oak tree.

Speaking for all of them, Sunny asked, "What animal is your Name Keeper?"

Chicago Red replied, "A bear."

CHAPTER NINE

Song at a Dark Moment

Since they had come into the Great Valley, the hunting and feeding were much improved. But one night the hunting turned bad. In their hunger, the cats became cranky and snappish.

Toward morning, they found a place to sleep under a laurel sumac at the corner of a freshly harvested grain field. "How much longer will it take us to get to those hills, Chicago Red?" BraveHeart whined. In his innocence, the fawn-and-brown seal point Siamese wanted to blame someone else for his misery.

"I don't know. I told you it would take days and days and days."

"We've already traveled days and days and days," the Siamese irritably pointed out.

Chicago Red thought for a moment. "It's really hard to say. But I'd guess we should arrive there about the time the moon is again just a little past full."

BraveHeart let out a disappointed groan.

"Look, boys, when I came this way, I was traveling alone and traveling fast. We're not. We were held up with that rainstorm the first four nights out. We've had to spend a lot of extra time while you guys learned to hunt. Then there was the night's travel we missed when Mister Backward was treed by those dogs."

"That wasn't my fault. I couldn't get down. Who'd ever think a cat would have to go down a tree backward," the Foldie said defensively. Embarrassed by the memory, he fell to grooming his ears with his left forepaw.

Chicago Red continued, "Then there were the two days we laid over while Practical helped the feral queen in the meadow with her new litter of kittens."

Practical looked indignant. "*Someone* had to bring her food, until she found a better place."

Chicago Red nodded his agreement. "Of course it was right of us to help. But my point is, there's no way to tell what may next interfere. It's getting cold, and we could get snow. Deep snow would really slow us up."

Still feeling low and wondering when they would see the foothills, they fell asleep under the sumac.

The next evening as they trudged along, Sunny thought about their growing irritation. It didn't all have to do with hunger. Most of it was caused by their sleep patterns. Back in Ridley Park, they were used to taking lots of short naps. But they couldn't do that in the wild.

They were becoming a bunch of tired, hungry, grumpy felines.

Nor did autumn's first cold spell a few days later improve anyone's mood. They had their winter coats by now, but the hunting stayed bad. One night when the cats had gone two days with almost nothing to eat, they came into a field of high grass. An outcropping of tall rocks thrust themselves into the sky above the dry, dead blades.

They were all beginning to feel the world was against them. They found no mice around the rocks. Everything seemed hard and unyielding. Whiskie climbed to the top of a large rock. The others followed. They sat together, high above the field, looking out over the farmland. Frost had formed across the fields and sparkled under the hard, autumn starlight. The Night Mother had all but disappeared. She would give them no light for many nights to come. Far away over the fields were a house and the outbuildings of a farm. A single light on a tall pole between the house and barn illuminated the buildings and surrounding yards. Cold and miserably hungry, they looked upon this stark scene with hard, condemning eyes. They felt abandoned under the big, star-spangled sky.

For just a moment, sitting on the rock, looking out across the frost-encrusted field, Sunny felt as if he had always lived here in this barren, lonely place. Ridley Park with its comforts and pleasantries was far, far away, almost forgotten. This cold, hard sky seemed to be the only roof he had ever known. These empty fields were where he had played as a kitten. Chicago Red and The Friendship were his only society. An empty despair set in and numbed him to the bone.

"I can't remember my own back yard," BraveHeart said. "It's so cold and lonely here."

"What a miserable place to spend your whole life," Practical grumped.

There's no doubt about it, Sunny thought. *We're getting in a bad way.*

Cold, hungry, and tired, they all slipped down from the rock and set off across the field, angling to miss the farm buildings.

About midnight it clouded up and a slow snow came down in large, soft, wet flakes. They had not trotted far before all their backs were covered with a light dusting of flakes like frosting on Christmas cookies. Through the rest of the night, they endured a cold soaking. The snow melted slowly, deeply penetrating each fur coat. By dawn they were as wretched as nine cats could be. Sunny did not know what to do about it. He had a feeling some of his friends, if offered the chance, would just quit.

They were a miserable lot. Their fur, especially on their legs, tails, and stomachs, was caked with mud. As they forced their way through a thorny thicket of wet chaparral, Sunny desperately tried to think of some way to pick up their spirits. He realized despair was setting in among his friends. Then he heard a voice lifted in song.

It was the song about the cat who brought the mail to Timaroola, the same song BraveHeart had sung in the alley their first night out. The voice was a deep baritone, full and harmonious.

> *It was the way he held his tail*
> *Said all the country 'round.*
> *Not his fur so plush and soft*
> *And not his stripes so brown.*
>
> *He was the cat with tail so dear,*
> *The cat without a single peer,*
> *The cat who brought the mail to Timaroola.*
>
> *There was one maiden in this town*
> *So fair and lovely*
> *That each man beat his breast and swore*
> *He'd have no one but she.*
> *"No," she said, with all her might.*

"The man I'll choose must be a sight
And learn to hold his tail just right,
Like the cat who brings the mail to Timaroola."

And now the men of Timaroola
Each have grown a tail.
And some are dark and some are white
And some are ghastly pale.

But none have got the slant just right.
And though they try with all their might,
None can get the darned thing right
Like the cat who brought the mail to Timaroola.

As the song was coming to an end, Sunny hurried to get out of the thorny brush so he could see who was singing. Sunny emerged from the thicket and waited with the others as the singer stepped into view. Sunny suddenly remembered where he had heard this voice before. In a cage in an alley, under a sentence of death, the singer had sung his heart out. The singer was Chicago Red.

"Why you have a beautiful voice," Sunny told the big moggie.

Chicago Red brightened. "You think so, little fellow? I love to sing, but sometimes I think it puts folks off, so I don't always do it. But I was feeling so bad back there I thought a little singing might cheer me up. At times like that, nothing will do but a good song."

The Duchess said, "Would you sing us another song? It might help us all."

"Why, boys, I'd be glad to and no joke."

They set off through a large wood and up a long, rock-strewn hill, with Chicago Red singing an old ballad. It was a song about a warm spring night that made them all forget they were cold and hungry. Soon they were lost in the soft, languid air of that magical moment.

The stars are a-twinkle in a magic sky.
The crickets sing cheer in the grass.
Sweetness descends on the world tonight
And enchants the world with a kiss.

The moon floats soft in a liquid sky.
The sweet dew comes down like grace.
Kindness descends on the land tonight
And gentles the world in this place.

The moon and the stars are lights above
That join as one on the grass.
Love descends on the land tonight
And blesses the world with a kiss."

Throughout the woods, Chicago Red's voice held them together as surely as if it had been a tether line between mountain climbers. Just as the night's storm rolled away to the west, rumbling like a departing army, and the sun peeked over the hills to the east, they came to a rock-strewn, wooded hillside that was like a small game preserve. The wood mice, moles, and chipmunks were everywhere. When they had finished eating and were ready for the day's sleep, the sun rose large and warm in the eastern sky. It was plain the early cold spell had passed and Indian Summer was coming on.

CHAPTER TEN

The Far Hills

The colors of autumn set in around them, splashing the landscape with warm yellows, oranges, and reds. Tiny white butterflies danced over ditch banks painted copper and rose. The next few nights were languid as Night Mother waxed larger and larger. One morning at dawn just before they settled down for the day's sleep, Chicago Red pointed out some blue bumps on the distant horizon. "There's our foothills," he said.

None of The Friendship had ever been near a mountain. They had no idea they would see the foothills miles and miles before they could set a paw on one. But as the days and nights passed, the blue bumps drew closer. Night Mother went past full, then into her dark phase.

Then came a night when a chill wind blew across their backs. By now most of the leaves had passed their brightest colors and fallen under paw. A single hill loomed ahead.

The Duchess was three or four cats back from Sunny. He listened to her as she taught BraveHeart about the moon, now shining on the horizon.

"Since that long ago time when we cats were worshipped as gods," said the Duchess, "the Night Mother has been good to us. But sometimes when she's been gone a long time, as she has been this past week, she stores up all her good luck and gives it to us in one night. On moon-luck-charged nights, the Mother is beautiful. Yes. Tonight is a night for moon luck."

Sunny smiled knowingly. None of them, of course, believed they *had* been gods. They all knew there's only one God, and He's certainly not a cat. The Duchess was simply talking about a time long ago. Cats harbor no superstitions when it comes to God, but they've always believed in moon luck.

Later when the Night Mother was directly overhead, soaring majestically among the stars, they came to a road that ran across their path and angled off to the north. Beyond this ribbon of asphalt grew a forest of Christmas trees, black beneath the moon.

"Boys," Chicago Red announced grandly, "this is the first of the foothills of The-Far-Away-Mountains-to-the-East. We have arrived."

They were suddenly quiet. It had been such a long trip. Could it really be true? None of them could believe they had actually and really arrived.

"You mean we've almost found Whiskie's Mom?" Gloriana asked, curiously tipping her grey-blue head.

Chicago Red nodded. "If Whiskie's vision was true, we're getting very close. But the distance remaining is a long, tiresome climb."

The Duchess looked around as if she expected to find a marker for the location. Finally, she simply asked, "What's the name of this place?"

"Just 'The Road,'" Chicago Red said.

Chicago Red started across the highway. The others followed. Sunny felt as if they'd just crossed an invisible line separating them from their pasts forever. The Great Valley lay behind like a conquered wasteland. The foothills of The-Far-Away-Mountains-to-the-East rose up to challenge them like a final and fearsome opponent. But no matter what, they had arrived. They were in the hills with Whiskie's Mom and her two kittens!

The highway disappeared as they plunged into a mountain wilderness. Even the air felt and smelled different. With each breath he took, the sharp, pungent fragrance of Christmas trees filled Sunny with new energy. The tree cover was thick overhead. But when he could glimpse the stars, they were crystal-bright. As they walked, the air rushed to his head. His mind felt light and airy but somehow clearer, too.

Gradually the slope of ground under paw turned steeper and trickier. The cats began struggling upward. With no path to follow, they stumbled up the uneven hill like sleepwalkers in a nightmare. With every step, Sunny tripped over a sharp rock or stepped on a round stone that rolled from under his paws. His legs grew tired and cramped. During their long journey, he had envisioned these foothills as cool and beautiful, as remote and idyllic as hills in a Bavarian fairy tale. Now he saw they were harsh, cruel, and inhospitable. *Why,* he pondered, *was I so eager to get here?*

Sunny's breathing became labored. His legs ached and cramped. It took every effort he could muster to lift one foot and set it in front of the other.

At last, they paused to rest and catch their breath. Sunny gratefully flopped down beside the Duchess and looked back the way they had come. The valley floor sparkled here and there with lights. Patches of lights twinkled far into the distance. *Could any of those lights be Ridley Park?* Sunny wondered. He felt small and pleasantly unimportant.

"Do you think any of those lights on the horizon might be home?" the Duchess asked, voicing the question in Sunny's mind.

"No," Chicago Red replied from his resting place lower on the hill. He turned his big head and looked up at her. "Ridley Park is far beyond even those farthest lights. But from here you get some idea how far we've come."

They all looked and thought about the long distance they had journeyed. Sunny was missing the comforts of home. Yesterday he dreamed he heard his Mom's can opener. The high-pitched, homey sound woke him, but it was only a Steller's jay. Now he lay on the hill, snug and warm with his tail wrapped over his nose, thinking about his life back home. How comfortable and pleasant it had been, especially on Sundays. He had always spent Sunday afternoon in quiet idleness in the family room of his big Georgian-style house with Blair-Mom and Jim-Dad, who would lie on their stomachs on the floor and share a large newspaper. "Read, read, read," Sunny would often think to himself, looking at Jim-Dad's broad highway of a back. Then Sunny would walk up that broad back and sit quietly between Jim-Dad's massive shoulders. He'd swing his tail thoughtfully to and fro, staring over Jim-Dad's head at the moving, crinkling paper until he could stand it no more. Then – pounce! Sunny would drop suddenly, like a terror, battling and crackling the paper into a senseless wad, while Blair-Mom, lying next to Jim-Dad, rolled on the rug in helpless laughter.

It was nice to have friends to play jokes on, Sunny thought to himself. *How warm and safe and comfortable my life once was. Why did I never see it before now?*

"I wonder what everyone in Ridley Park is doing tonight?" Whiskie mewed longingly.

"Probably wondering where we are," BraveHeart replied.

"No," Practical moaned sadly. "I don't think so."

"Of course they are," BraveHeart snapped. "They're our moms. I'll bet they worry about us all the time."

"Let's face it, we've been gone a long, long time. I imagine everyone has given up hope we'll return. They have no idea what happened to us. That must be sad for them. But if they knew what we're doing, I think they'd be proud because we're doing the right thing."

They lay in silence, resting. After some time, Sunny felt his strength renewed, his energy recharged. Chicago Red said, "We can't dawdle here all night. Let's get going. We can climb many hills before dawn."

Which is exactly what they did. They spent the rest of the night in a vertical world. Something crazy seemed to have happened to the earth, as if it had been tipped on its side. They never trotted on the level, but always climbed up, up, and up. Just before dawn Sunny reached a new level of weariness. His mind began to spin with fatigue. His legs were like lead, and his tongue felt like dry sandpaper against his parched lips.

Dawn found them on the wooded crown of a small hill at the base of a gigantic rocky cliff. The immense cliff towered high above them, blotting out any sign of hills or mountains beyond. Scaling the giant cliff would be impossible. They'd have to travel around it. Too exhausted to bother appeasing their growling stomachs, they collapsed together into a helter-skelter pile among the bare roots of a great, heavy-limbed sycamore and fell into a deep sleep.

CHAPTER ELEVEN

A Second Message from the Moon

When Chicago Red and The Friendship awakened in the chill evening air, their breaths made little clouds in front of their whiskers. Gloriana was missing! Just as they had begun to get up a party to search for her, she came dancing back into camp.

"I've found a whole river of the most scrumptious water I've ever tasted. It's deliciously cold," she announced merrily.

Being very thirsty, they instantly forgave the Russian Blue for scaring them by wandering off without telling anyone. She proudly led them to her treasure, a broad and leaping river rushing down out of the hills. Bouncing off rocks, the water jumped clear, cold, and sparkling in the twilight. The cats crouched on the dark bank, thrust their muzzles into the bracing water, and lapped up their fill.

"Well, it's time for us all to get on the trail, "Chicago Red finally announced. "We'll follow the stream." He quickly started off along the bank.

"Just a minute, Chicago Red," Sunny called, bringing the big moggie to a halt.

"What?" Chicago Red demanded, irritated at being checked.

"Your advice up until now has been invaluable," Sunny said carefully. "None of us knew how to get to these hills, and we thank you for showing us the way. Also, you have been here before, so we are all counting on your wise advice in the future. But as to the exact path we should take right now — well, I think Whiskie, not you, should decide that."

Chicago Red stood his ground. He gave Sunny such an even look the whole Friendship thought fur was about to fly. But, suddenly, the red-and-white moggie relented. Turning abruptly, he returned to The Friendship. His tail was straight up and not kinked on the end, so they all knew everything was just fine with him.

"Of course," he said magnanimously. "Whiskie has the gift."

"What do you think, Whiskie?" Hildy asked. "Should we follow this river into the hills or not?"

Whiskie thought a moment. After a long pause, he shook his head. In a faltering voice, he hesitantly decided, "No. There's nothing special about this river. But then I also feel it's wrong to leave it. I don't think the river itself matters. But I think not leaving does matter."

"Well, make up your mind!" Hildy snapped, plainly irritated by Whiskie's wavering.

"He did make up his mind," Practical said. "Whiskie says we should follow the river."

"And what if once we set out along the bank he decides we *shouldn't* follow it?"

"Then we won't follow it," Practical retorted. "What on earth is wrong with you, Hildy? You know it's Whiskie's job to find the way. That means we go with *all* his decisions, not just the ones we like. We'll stick with him, no matter how many times he changes his mind. You know that."

Hildy took a deep breath and let it out slowly. "Sorry. I guess I'm getting impatient, but you needn't scold me, Practical."

"Well, I guess I'm getting impatient, too," Lady Practical apologized back. "But we have to trust Whiskie to find the way."

They headed along the river like aimless vagabonds, letting the leaping water direct them. They climbed higher and higher into the hills and the night. Sadly, the riverbanks were mostly solid rock, and the hunting was lousy.

Finally at dawn, they came to a rocky hillside looming above the river and providing regular outcroppings like little lean-tos. Cats love being up high. But they also love being hidden. The leaning rocks were perfect. To their delight, the rocky hillside was alive with small game. After eating their fill, they each chose a sheltering rock and curled up for the day's sleep. All in all, it was a perfect lodging. They could have done no better if they'd called ahead for reservations.

For the next two nights, they followed the river high into the hills. By now they were so weary they sometimes nodded off as they traveled, falling asleep on their feet. Regularly, they stopped to freshen themselves with the cold, clear water flashing by on its way to the valley. The icy water rushed madly down the mountainside, leaping and crashing recklessly over rocks in a wild uproar. Sunny thought The-Far-Away-Mountains-to-the-East must surely soon run dry.

Shortly after midnight, on their third night following the river, The Friendship and Chicago Red came to a wide, deep pool at the base of a waterfall. Tilting their heads back, they looked up and saw two more waterfalls towering above the first. Their eyes followed the water down, down, down as it slipped swiftly across slick black rocks. Shimmering and glistening like Christmas tinsel in the moonlight, the falls leaped out into space and crashed with a deafening roar into the pool. Standing by the pool, the cats felt a steady cool spray on their faces.

Fortunately, the climb up past the three falls was easier than it looked. A clear path led in gentle switchbacks from the base of the first falls toward the top of the third one. At times, the path widened enough so that they could walk two or three abreast. Unfortunately, a more soaking path they could not have found. It was a wet, chilly, depressing climb. They were all in low spirits, and the wet dark only deepened their misery.

As they climbed alongside the third waterfall, Whiskie suddenly asked in a quiet voice, "Sunny, do you think a dream about the moon could be important?"

"Maybe. What was the dream?"

"We were all in this big tree not far from a farm. I was asleep. The moon came down and sat on the branch right next to me. She shone so brightly I woke up. Then the Queen of the Night said to me, 'On the back of a friend, your Mom will find freedom.'"

"That wasn't a dream. That was a vision."

"I think so, too. It was too strong to be only a dream. But I've thought and thought, and I can't make out what it means."

"It sounds as if one of us is going to rescue her. But that can't be right because we're too small. None of us can carry her on our backs."

Whiskie just look puzzled. "I agree. None of us could possibly rescue her."

Thus, it was decided: Whiskie's dream sounded important, but it probably meant nothing. They all felt relieved. If Whiskie was getting meaningless messages from the moon, maybe the blood he saw on the animals at the farm also meant nothing.

Just before dawn, they reached the top of the third waterfall, and Whiskie decided the river looked dry.

"Dry? What do you mean dry?" Hildy snapped.

"I guess I mean dead. Isn't that what dead water would be-- dry?"

"I never knew water was alive," Hildy grumbled. "So how could it look dead?"

"That's not fair," Whiskie retorted peevishly. "You've all asked me to psi-trail to find my Mom. I did not even know I could do it before we started out. Now I seem to be doing it. But I can only tell you what I feel. I don't know what these feelings mean. Up until right here, this river looked alive. It seemed to be going somewhere. Now it looks dead. Dry. I think we should leave it."

"If you ask me, I think we should leave you," Hildy replied irritably.

"Now wait a minute," Chicago Red put in. "Whiskie may be onto something. We're looking for a deserted farm, and I've been all along this river far up into these hills. There's no farm along it. That's one reason I wanted to leave the river a few days back. Maybe Whiskie's right. How about it, Sunny?"

Sunny did not know how to support or dispute Whiskie's claims. He knew Whiskie was running on faith, and faith meant you were trusting in the mystery of love as your guide. So Sunny kept his silence. They trotted a bit farther along the river bank until Whiskie came to a narrow path he was certain they had to follow. The path led away from the river, into the hills. They took it and turned their tails on the river.

The third night past Three Falls, they traveled in a cold mountain rain. The trail ran with water, at times almost up to their knees. The areas just off the trail were slippery with soft mud.

Since he knew nothing of this part of the foothills, Chicago Red kept moving out ahead of them to scout out the trail. Once after he had been gone for nearly an hour, Sunny looked up and saw him standing like a pillar in the rain on the edge of the trail far ahead of them. The big moggie's fur looked soaked, but Sunny suspected that beneath that thick coat of his, Chicago Red was probably dry.

As The Friendship came up to him, Chicago Red called out in a dire voice, "Boys, just ahead is a clearing. I want to show you something you need to see."

What he wanted to show them were owl pellets.

The ground under the canopy of cottonwood leaves was almost dry and littered with dozens of owl pellets. The pellets looked to Sunny like little round cakes of dried grass. Inside each cake were hard things Sunny couldn't define. He gave one pellet a hard poke with his paw. It fell apart. Out rolled a small, partly crushed cat's skull. He jumped back in horror.

"What've you got there, Sunny?" Hildy asked.

"Ugh!" she exclaimed, which attracted Practical. Soon they were all gathered around, looking at the crushed skull of what had once been a living cat wandering through these mountains, hunting and eating much as they were doing.

Sunny's stomach suddenly felt queasy. The owl, Chicago Red had told them, spit out these pellets under its roosting tree. So at this very moment, they were all standing under an owl's home, and this owl liked to eat cats. A prickly feeling like static electricity ran up Sunny's spine.

Sunny glanced at the others. The hackles on all his friends' backs were standing erect.

"Let's get out of here," the Duchess said with a shudder.

But Chicago Red said, "Don't worry, boys. Owls spend the night hunting. Even in rain like this, they don't stick around home. Probably the safest place to be right now is under this tree."

Even so, they all felt greatly relieved as they moved away from that awful tree. As they trudged on into the night, Sunny could not put the skull out of his mind. *What kind of a cat had it been? A kitten? A mother? A prowling tom? A feral cat who'd lived its whole life in these hills?*

A sudden image of a large attack bird, swiftly and silently dropping out of the sky, coming at him with huge feet and razor-sharp claws at the ends of gargantuan toes, made the thrill like static electricity run up his spine again. He trudged on, unsettled and nervous.

CHAPTER TWELVE

The Farm in the Valley

They sloshed silently along the slick, muddy trail. Much later, the rain stopped and the clouds blew away on a cold night wind. As they crossed a broad clearing atop a large knoll, the stars hung bright in a cold sky. The Night Mother was a thick crescent low in the east. Chicago Red left again to scout the trail ahead.

Suddenly, Sunny saw a great bird diving out of the sky.

"Look out, Practical!" Sunny cried.

The British Shorthair spun quickly to face her attacker. She had no chance. The talons missed her spine, but the deadly hooks closed in front of her face, hitting her like a punch. She flipped backwards, ears over tail, and lay perfectly still.

The owl rose on silent wings above the clearing. He wheeled ponderously. Then he streaked down like a jet fighter toward Practical's lifeless body. The owl did not see Chicago Red return, so the bird had no defense for the red-and-white thunderbolt that launched itself at him. Chicago Red met the owl in mid-air and hit him an explosive blow, blasting a cloud of feathers around them like a bomb. Owl and cat rolled sideways in the air. They hit the ground several feet from the brown tabby, who lay still and quiet in the cold mountain grass.

The great bird, struggling for survival, staggered to his feet. Lifting his huge wings, he took to the air and soared toward the moon.

Chicago Red dashed across the clearing to Practical. He and the others crowded about her. They were overcome with grief.

"She didn't even see him coming," BraveHeart cried. Tears rolled down his Siamese cheeks.

"She was just middle-aged – only seven years old!" said Gloriana, choking back a sob.

Just then, Practical opened her eyes and glanced around in a glassy daze.

"She's alive!" BraveHeart shouted.

But for how long? Sunny thought to himself.

Chicago Red bent tenderly over the brown tabby. "There's a farm just ahead, over a few hills," he said gently. "I don't know if it's the farm were looking for. I was coming back to tell you about it when I saw the owl. We could set up a sort of field hospital bed there for you. Do you think you can make it that far?"

Silent, Practical lay down again and closed her eyes.

After much discussion, they got their groggy friend up and headed for the hilltop where they could look down on the farm. Once they saw the farm, they would decide what to do.

BraveHeart and the Duchess, one on each side of the brown tabby, helped her stumble along the trail.

The hill was steep. By the time The Friendship reached the top and looked down on the farm, the moon had climbed high in the sky.

Standing on the crest of the high hill, Sunny studied the farm carefully. His heart sank. Could this be the place they had journeyed so far to find? Had they gone tired and hungry, suffering miserably, just to reach this shabby collection of ramshackle buildings? He felt nothing for the farm but intense loathing.

The buildings were loosely scattered over a few acres of a broad valley overlooked by the jagged peaks of The-Far-Away-Mountains-to-the East. A broad, shallow river snaked from the mountains and circled behind the farm buildings, where it cut a deep gorge. A small, rag-tag dirt road passed in front of the thickly weeded front yard of a one-story, grey clapboard house with a sagging roof and a leaning chimney. The road wound past the house and ended near an old back porch, which had lost most of its shingles. At the foot of a pair of rickety steps sat a large metal trash can, overflowing with garbage. Parked several feet from the steps in a little, dusty parking lot was a black van. To the west of the van stood a shed completely surrounded by runs made of chain-link fences. Inside the runs, several large dogs moved restlessly about.

"Dogs! They have dogs!" Sunny exclaimed anxiously.

"But look – they're kept in a kennel," Chicago Red pointed out. "That's good for us."

North of the kennels stretched a barnyard full of tall weeds, coarse and broad-leafed. A beaten-down footpath led through the weeds, past a small barn, across the barnyard, and out into a large, broad pasture beyond the house and alongside the road. Once painted red, the barn had long since faded to a weathered grey. The barnyard was marked off by decayed and leaning fence posts from which ran strands of wire, sagging and broken.

Sunny shuddered and turned to look at Practical. She remained stretched out on her side, her eyes closed. He recalled Dr. Vivian Blaise, the beloved veterinarian in Ridley Park. All cats and their moms adored Dr. Blaise. Oh, how he wished she were here.

Whiskie came up and stood by Sunny's shoulder. He looked sorrowfully down on the farm. Sunny sensed his anxiety.

"We don't know yet if your Mom's there or not, Whiskie."

Whiskie was silent a moment. Then he said, "It's a nasty place, isn't it?"

Sunny didn't know what to say. On all the farms they had passed coming across the valley, lights were always on at night, making the buildings look like bright little islands in a black sea. But the pole lamp between this house and the kennels was unlit, as if these men embraced the darkness. Could this be the Farm of Blood in Whiskie's dream?

Urging Practical to her feet, the cats moved down the steep switchbacks to a meadow filled with rabbit brush. Taking care to avoid the house, they angled to the right of the weathered barn. No human was stirring at this hour. So no one saw nine cats come down from the hills and cross to the river. Those at the farm slept on peacefully under the hard stars and crescent moon, unaware they had just been occupied by the enemy.

CHAPTER THIRTEEN

Sunny Finds His Wild Voice

They crossed the gently flowing river on a tangled pile of driftwood and ascended to the other side. At the top of the bank, they came upon a large black oak that still had its summer leaves. Sunny and Chicago Red walked around the tree, looking it up and down.

"Yes," Sunny finally said. "We can use this tree as our headquarters. We'll call it Oak House. It's far enough from the farmhouse that no one will notice us here."

As some of the cats settled into Oak House, the others went to look for a place to put Practical. BraveHeart found a perfect spot just beyond Oak House, up a little hill under a sturdy buckeye bush. They tucked the brown tabby into a nest safely out of sight from any evil passing eyes. She immediately drifted into a deep sleep, or maybe a coma, nobody knew which. Mister Backward and the Duchess volunteered to stay with her. The others set out immediately to search for Whiskie's Mom.

"Our worst worries are the dogs' noses," Sunny observed. "They'll pick up our scent. Then they'll bark, and the humans will know we're here."

"The humans won't believe the dogs. Not if we make ourselves invisible," Chicago Red replied mysteriously. He promptly led them back across the river toward the kennel shed.

Standing in tall weeds at the edge of the barnyard, they peeped out at the kennel shed. It has several little doors, all closed and locked tight. Long, narrow dog runs completely encircled the shed. Four gates in the dog runs could be opened or closed. They were standing open, but the dog runs were empty. To their right, west of the dog runs, was a smaller shed with raspberry bushes growing beside it. A strange, sickeningly sweet but familiar scent came from the shed.

"Puppies," Chicago Red said, identifying the scent. "The mothers with puppies must be kept in there."

"Come on, Sunny," he added as he moved toward the empty dog runs.

Sunny capered after him. A few feet from the chain-link fence, Chicago Red sat back on his haunches. Sunny plopped down beside him. "What do we do now?" the American Shorthair asked.

"Wait for him to see us," the big moggie replied.

Then Sunny saw there *was* a dog in the kennel runs. A large German shepherd lay silently alone in a corner, ignoring them.

"Hello there," Chicago Red called out cheerily.

The dog lay still, staring directly at them. Sunny suddenly realized the dog had known they were here all along. "Aren't you going to tell the men we're here?"

The dog muttered, "It makes no difference to me if they know you're here."

Sunny found the dog's voice disturbing. It contained an ancient misery, a black despair so heavy Sunny felt its crushing weight. No animal– cat, dog, or horse – could long stand up with that depression on its back. What was wrong with him? Then Chicago Red did a strange thing. He began to sing:

Let me tell you a story of a dog I once knew,
Who gave his heart in a love that was true.
His heart was good but his eyes they were not,
For he fell in love with an old flower pot.

Now this is a song that makes dogs very angry. Even the most placid of them can be driven to fits of rage when they hear it. That's because dogs are proud of their ability to love. Indeed, they see it as their greatest strength. And why shouldn't they – for it is their glory. But the implication of the song is that dogs, unlike cats, love so indiscriminately they often look foolish, and their devotions lead to nothing. At least that's how dogs have come to regard this particular song. And cats know this and have been taunting dogs with it for ages.

The old dog just lay there. He stared voicelessly at the two cats. Chicago Red nudged Sunny with his shoulder. Together they sang:

His heart was good but his eyes they were not,
For he fell in love with an old flower pot.

"Hey, hey," shouted a voice from the other side of the kennel shed. "What's going on?"

Around a corner of the shed pranced a young dog, white with black patches. He had a vicious air about him, and Sunny was grateful a strong fence stood between them.

Chicago Red sang on:

He swore he'd be true for all of his life
And took a clay pot for his true wedded wife.

Then together he and Sunny sang,

His heart was good but his eyes they were not,
And he fell in love with an old flower pot.

The black-and-white mongrel flew threateningly up to the fence and howled out: "Why you mealie-mouthed hairball! Bark, bark! You pile of scat! Bark, bark! I ought'ta bark, bark! And bark, bark, bark! You know who I am?"

Chicago Red began washing his face with one insouciant paw. He stopped for a second, pausing with the paw in front of his face. "Why, yes. You're the hound dog who couldn't see beyond his own nose and married a ceramic bowl."

"Why you Grrrrr! I'm no hound dog. Grrrr-rrr-rrrr. Name's Grrrrrrr! Jugular! Rrr-r-r-Rowf! Fighting dog. Bark, bark, and grrrrr-ark, ark, bark, bark!"

Just then four more dogs emerged from behind the kennel shed, led by a dun-colored brute.

"Ark! Ark! Eat off his head! Eat off his head! Bark! Bark!" said the dun-colored brute. He was followed by three other dogs: a short, squat, bull-dog type with a brown coat; a tattered long-haired, black-and-tan hound; and a grey Russian-wolfhound creature, who snapped his jaws at the cats.

"R-r-r-rowf!"Jugular introduced them. "This is my ark! bark! friend, rowf! rowf! Markee Day Sod! He wants to eat off your head."

Jugular then turned to the other three.

"Ark! Ark! Bark! Bark! Rowlf! Rowlf! Meet Blood Hungry and Captain Blood Ark! Ark! Rowlf! and our last friend Ark! Ark! Whose name Bark! Bark! is Snap-Snap."

Just then the backyard pole light came on. Two men came out of the house. They hurried down the back porch steps past the overfull metal garbage can. One carried a flashlight. The other carried what looked to Sunny like a short stick. They crossed to the kennel. The flashlight beam danced over the ground and flicked and flashed about the kennel runs. The light played over Jugular, jumping frantically, barking loudly at nothing. The two cats had fled back to their hiding place with the other cats in the weeds.

Giving it up, both men retreated across the weedy yard, up the steps, and back into the house. The pole light went out.

The old German shepherd put his chin on his paws, closed his eyes, and said nothing.

"Did you see what that man without the flashlight was carrying?" Chicago Red asked.

"A stick, wasn't it?" observed Sunny.

"No. It was a gun. Guns are dangerous. Very dangerous. If they have a gun and they can see us when they come out of the house, they can kill us from the back porch."

"How can they do that?" Sunny asked. It was hard to believe.

"Don't know. But they can. I can only tell you their guns don't work very well if the men have to act quickly. And you can't let a man point a gun at you. Not directly at you."

Sunny soon understood what Chicago Red had in mind when he said they would make themselves invisible. Three more times they sang to the dogs, and three more times the men came out of the house, with the flashlight and the gun, but found nothing. Sunny especially liked the verse that went:

Of the offspring produced then this was the sum:
One was a hound dog and one was a mum.
His heart was good but his eyes they were not.
He was forever wed to an old flower pot.

Once the flashlight accidentally flashed across the face of the man with the gun, and Sunny's blood ran cold. The man had an ugly, puffy face, blank in its cruelty, with little, hard eyes that seemed to project hate. Sunny shivered. He hoped that if he were caught, it would not be by that man. Both men once again went back into the house and turned off the pole light.

It was then that Sunny and Chicago Red made a grave mistake. They were watching for the pole light to come on before retreating to the weed patch. But their next time out, the men did not turn on the light. Before either cat knew it, the men were almost upon them.

Chicago Red leaped into the night. But Sunny's escape was cut off by the two men, who appeared suddenly between him and the weed patch where The Friendship was hiding. Finding his flight cut off, Sunny froze.

"Jump, Sunny, jump!" Chicago Red called to him from the weeds. His voice had an odd tone that Sunny found strange, thrilling– and frightening. Just as the light beam played over the spot where he stood, Sunny jumped. He landed in the raspberry bushes next to the puppy shed and instantly knew he was in serious trouble. He was hidden, but he couldn't get out of the raspberry patch without the men spotting him. Worse yet, he knew that once they saw him, they would use that terrible gun.

Not knowing how the gun would kill him only added to his terror.

From somewhere in the darkness, Chicago Red called, "Can you see them, Sunny?"

"No," Sunny replied in sudden desperation. He was astounded to hear himself using the same tone of voice Chicago Red was using. It came naturally and somehow felt just right. He added, "I'm in the raspberry bushes by the puppy shed. At the end closest to Oak House."

"They're coming toward you right now. Wait. When I tell you, move quickly but quietly toward the other end of the shed."

Sunny waited. He realized he and his friend were getting away with something dangerous. He was terrified. His heart raced. Blood thundered in his ears.

"All right. Now, Sunny! Run to the other end."

Sunny ran. He briefly glimpsed the men's feet and a flicker of light as he passed them by. Then he was at the other end of the shed, and the men were behind him.

Eventually the men went back inside. Sunny and Chicago Red joined up in front of the kennel, where they once again sang to the dogs, taunting them into creating another uproar. But this time the men, disgusted with being awakened too many times in the middle of the night, did not come out. After a while the rowdy dogs saw their barking would bring no one. They sat down behind the fence, stared at Chicago Red and Sunny, and licked their muzzles.

Sunny said, "Congratulations, Chicago Red. I see what you mean. We're invisible."

The two cats swaggered away from the kennel runs, boldly singing,

Now of their offspring, this was the sum:
One was a hound dog and one was a mum.

They joined the rest of the Friendship in the tall weeds beside the barn.

"Chicago Red, how could we be talking so loudly and not be heard?" Sunny wondered.

"We were talking in our wild voices. As kittens, we used to talk in our wild voices a lot. After a while we forgot we have a wild voice. Being out here on your own, your wild voice is becoming stronger, and finally you responded to me in it.

"What is this wild voice exactly?"

Chicago Red shook his head. "I only know humans and dogs can't hear anything we say in it. Hearing mine, you automatically responded in your wild voice. Now it will come more natural and more often to you. Your wild voice is the voice of your *Meena-Ooma*. If you're ever called upon to talk to your *Meena-Ooma*, speak in that voice and it will hear you more clearly."

"You were taking an awful chance, weren't you?"

"With most cats, yes. But, Sunny, I've come to know you. You have a very powerful wild side. All of you do, or you wouldn't be here. But there's one other thing you should know. And that is, once you've spoken in your wild voice, it means you've found your *Meena-Ooma*, and you're ready to name it. You must choose your secret name soon, Sunny. So forget your show business ambitions. Your *Meena-Ooma* is your wild self. It has nothing to do with your pride or ambitions. It's the real you."

CHAPTER FOURTEEN

The Beast in the Dark

In the cool pre-dawn air at the edge of the driveway in which the black van was parked, Sunny stood and looked at the big, decaying clapboard house. They had decided not to go back to Oak House, but to begin searching immediately for Whiskie's Mom. During the couple hours left before dawn, they might find her. If she wasn't here, they needed to know, so they could move on as soon as Practical was able to travel. The chill night sky above the foothills shone rich with stars, which Sunny no longer found distant nor alien. *Your Meena-Ooma is your wild self. It's the real you.* He felt part of the stars and they were part of him. He belonged here in the wild foothills. He was not far from home. He was home.

Chicago Red had gone to search the dog kennel. Hildy and Gloriana were searching the barn. Whiskie had asked Sunny to look around the house, in case she was there. At first, Sunny had protested. The house was the most obvious place for her to be. Why didn't Whiskie want to look there for himself? Whiskie sat down on his haunches. His head dropped forward and his tail lay listlessly on the gravel driveway. His ears drooped and his whiskers were flattened against his cheeks. Even his fur seemed to lie close against his skin as if he were trying to become small and inconspicuous. There was fear in Whiskie's voice as he said, "The animals here have blood on them." If this *was* the Farm of Blood in his dream and there was blood on his Mom, he didn't want to see it. So, Sunny had agreed to search the house.

Sighing with resignation, Sunny began to move through the high weeds and grass in the side yard. This was really going to irritate his sensitive whiskers. At home, he would not even put his muzzle in a bowl if his whiskers bumped the inside. Cats find anything that touches their whiskers irritating. But here he had no choice. Using his head to force the plants apart, he stalked forward, burrowing through the unmown weeds. As he moved forward, the weeds snapped at his face. He could not see beyond the weeds and grass, so he kept his bearings mostly by memory.

As he plowed through the weeds toward the porch, he thought to himself, *Is this the deserted farm Chicago Red was talking about? It looks so old, it must have been here years before Chicago Red spent that winter up here in the mountains. But whether or not it's the farm Whiskie saw in his dream is another matter. The only way we'll know is by looking.*

He decided to check the back porch for the scent of either Edeline or her kittens. Whiskie's Mom wore perfume he liked, and he might be able to detect that. At the corner of the dilapidated back porch, he emerged from the grass and weeds, near the overfull metal garbage can.

Just as he rounded the corner of the porch, a huge and horrible shadow suddenly reared up with surprising agility from behind the garbage can and towered over him.

Sunny instantly saw the dark shadow was a shaggy beast with sharp claws on the ends of heavy paws. It had huge jaws and teeth half as long as his forelegs. The sudden appearance of this monstrous brute hit Sunny like an electric shock. He had no time to run. Just then the monster used one of its great forepaws to topple the overfull garbage can, which came crashing toward Sunny. The garbage exploded from the can, and Sunny had to jump fast to get out of the way.

At the roots of the hairs all over a cat's body are tiny erector muscles that go into action when a cat is frightened or angry. These muscles cause a cat's hairs to stand on end. You only have a few of these erector muscles on the back of your neck. Imagine how it must feel to a cat for the hair all over its body to stand suddenly on end. Well, that's exactly what happened to Sunny at the moment the garbage can clattered toward him. He jumped, arched his back, and bristled his crest and tail. He hissed and spat hot breath at the clumsy brute.

The great beast, standing on its hind legs with one weighty forepaw resting on the side of the garbage can, looked down at the tiny, defiant cat.

"Why are you hissing at me, little fellow?" the beast asked with strange sincerity.

Something in the beast's manner caused Sunny to realize that, other than getting stepped on, he was in no real danger. He lowered his back and tail, un-bristled his whole body, and backed away a few paces. But just to be on the safe side, he mentally measured the distance, in jumps, to the tall weeds and grass at the corner of the porch.

"Hissing at me hurts my feelings," the brute said. Sunny detected wounded pride in the great beast's voice.

"Well — sorry. You frightened me. I didn't mean anything personal by it. Hissing is just what I do when I'm scared, like purring when I'm content."

The huge animal did not respond. Instead, he leaned his body forward. Thrusting his right forepaw into the half-spilled garbage, he groped for something to eat. He dragged trash out of the garbage can and began going through the refuse, grunting heavily.

Suddenly, the brute stopped rummaging through the cast-off food. He looked down at Sunny.

"I'd hiss at me, too, if I saw me here." The beast rolled out half a watermelon. He sighed and shook his head in resignation. "Look at me. I used to be big, strong, and fast. I could get food anywhere. Now I'm old and weak. I have to raid garbage cans to get dinner. I'm hungry most of the time, little fellow."

He angrily swept the garbage can to one side with a mighty blow of his paw. As powerful as the beast was, Sunny thought he understood his sorrow. It was the sorrow of aging. He had seen it even among the cats of Ridley Park.

The beast dropped his heavy rump on the ground next to the steps, let out a despairing moan, and stared morosely off into the darkness. Sunny suddenly felt sorry for him. He climbed the stairs and sat on the top step next to the bear's face so he could look him directly in the eye.

"I'm sure you mean what you say," Sunny told him. "And I'm sure you're not feeling sorry for yourself. But you *are* still very strong. It would be wonderful if I had your strength."

He suddenly realized that if he had this beast's strength, he could simply knock down all the doors in the place, find the stolen humans, and carry them off. But he was just a little cat.

The big bear looked at him as if some of his pride had been restored. He sniffed at Sunny with his long, brown muzzle. "I'm Gar," he said. "What's your name, little fellow?"

"Sunny."

Gar said, "You're not from around here. But something about your scent is familiar."

Gar turned from him and looked off into the night, as if he were trying to remember something. Sunny did not disturb him. They sat silently for a few moments, with the big bear on the ground thinking and little cat on the top step, level with his head. After a few moments of reflecting, the shaggy beast — in sudden recognition — whirled with eyes wide open to Sunny.

Seeing the light in his eyes, Sunny said, "You've just thought of what's familiar about me, haven't you?'

And the bear said something that astounded Sunny.

Gar said, "Yes. Chicago Red."

CHAPTER FIFTEEN

Whiskie Finds His Mom

Sunny headed back toward Oak House. He hadn't found Whiskie's Mom. *This must be the wrong farm,* he thought to himself with disappointment. He crossed the river and came up under Oak House.

Mister Backward raced down the hill from Practical's nest to meet him. "Chicago Red found Whiskie's Mom!!!" the sweet-faced Foldie exclaimed. He jumped up and down with excitement. His long, tapered tail stood straight on end with joy.

"What?? Really?? Wow!!! Where? Where is she?"

Mister Backward quickly led Sunny back to where the cats were gathered around Practical. The brown tabby was awake, finishing off a meal. Her eyes were bright and clear.

"Is it true?" Sunny asked Chicago Red. "Did you find Whiskie's Mom and her two kittens?"

Chicago Red nodded. "They're in the dog kennel. The dogs are guarding her."

"Locked up in a kennel?" Sunny was outraged. No kidnappers could be that mean.

"With only two thin blankets. Their only light is a candle," Chicago Red reported sadly.

"But there's no blood on her and no blood on any of the dogs," Whiskie said. His tail was straight on end, a sign he, too, was happy.

"I think I can explain that," Hildy boomed.

They all looked at her.

"This farm is run by Wolfgang Roach. He's the one who kidnapped Whiskie's Mom."

Groans of despair went up from the show cats.

Chicago Red looked around in confusion. "Who's Wolfgang Roach?"

"A very cruel man who hates all animals," Sunny explained. "He teaches animals to fight, which is against the law. Whiskie's Mom once turned him into the police, and he went to prison."

"Well, he's at it again," Hildy said. "All the animals on this farm, except the cats in the barn, are trained to fight: horses, dogs, and fighting cocks. The big birds Whiskie saw in his dream are chickens."

"How could a chicken fight a horse?" Mister Backward asked.

Suppressing a laugh, Hildy explained, "Chickens don't fight horses, silly. Each animal fights its own kind. That's why Whiskie saw blood. They're all fighters. Other men come from all over the world to get Roach's animals because they're so vicious. He has one dog, a German shepherd named Top Dog, who has never lost a fight."

Suddenly Sunny remembered the scarred old German shepherd with his heavy despair.

"Roach also has a stallion, Hudrughynhyn, who has a stall in the barn. I met him tonight," Hildy continued. "He has fought and beaten a dozen other horses. Yes. Whiskie was right. The animals here *are* all covered with blood."

"What about the cats in the barn?"

"There are five of them. The men have not even named them. They just go by 'The Tabby Cat,' 'The Black Cat,' 'The Calico Cat,' 'The Grey Cat,' and 'The Tiger Cat.'"

"They must not be very territorial," Sunny observed. "I've seen none of their markings around this farm. Have you?"

No one had, neither scat nor scratches.

"That's because of the mean men," Hildy said. "This farm belongs to them, so the cats keep a low profile. But enough of this. We have to get Whiskie and Mister Backward to Whiskie's Mom right away. If we wait until daylight, the men will see us. Let's go!" Weeks earlier, as they crossed the Great Valley, Mister Backward had decided to stay with Whiskie and help comfort the humans when the other cats returned home. Backward just loved the kittens.

"Come on, boys," Chicago Red said. "I'll show you how to get past those dogs and inside the kennel shed. It's as easy as catching a dead mouse."

As they crossed the river, Sunny thought to himself, *I guess all our troubles are over. We've done everything we set out to do. We've helped Whiskie find his Mom and her two kittens. Mission accomplished! We'll leave Whiskie and Backward here. In a few days, the rest of us will head home to Ridley Park.* He felt jubilant, and yet somehow sad at the same time. It's always hard to end a good adventure.

"See that chain-link roof," Chicago Red whispered as they stood in the patch of weeds beside the puppy shed, looking out at the kennel. "We can cross over that and slip in between the walls and roof of the shed. Inside, I saw the three humans asleep on the dirt floor. The dogs never even knew I was there."

They waited until all the dogs were on the other side of the shed. Dashing for the kennel-run fence, they scurried up the side, across the top, and inside the shed. All the gates in the runs around the shed were standing wide open so the dogs could guard the prisoners. If Whiskie's Mom or her kittens tried to escape, one of the vicious dogs could get at them and tear them to pieces. Sunny shuddered.

Inside, the shed was pitch-black. But with their keen cat eyes, they could see clearly. Looking down from the rafters, Sunny spied Whiskie's Mom and her two kittens curled asleep under a shabby, grey blanket on the dirt floor. The reeking scent of dog was everywhere. It even seemed to come out of the walls. Sunny immediately missed a scent he had been looking forward to — the perfume Whiskie's Mom always wore. He liked the smell of perfumes, colognes, and hand lotions, as all cats do, but he especially loved Whiskie's Mom's perfume. It smelled like jasmine and lilacs.

Two-by-four boards made little ledges at various heights all the way down the wall. Whiskie used these short ledges like a stairway to descend from the rafter to the floor. Mister Backward climbed halfway down the wall and sat on a ledge, just waiting for the moment he could rush to the two human kittens he loved best in the world. Chicago Red stayed up on the rafters near Sunny.

Sitting beside Chip's face, Whiskie reached out his small, dainty forepaw and gently patted the boy on the nose, as he sometimes did at home when he wanted Chip to wake up. Chip stirred, but slept on. Whiskie patted him again. This time, Chip awakened. He turned sleepily toward his mother in the darkness. His stirring woke Edeline.

"What is it, Chip?" she asked.

Chip rubbed his eyes with his fists and sat up. "I just had a dream, Mother, that we were back home and Whiskie was trying to wake me up."

Edeline reached out and took her son gently in her arms.

"It's all right, honey. It's been a long time. But I'm sure your father has not given up and he will never let the police give up. We'll be found. You'll see."

Even as she said this, she realized she no longer believed it herself. When they were first kidnapped, Edeline had high hopes of being rescued. Now she could barely keep up her children's spirits. Her own hopes had sunk out of sight long ago.

Whiskie rubbed his head against Chip's thigh.

"Mother? Whiskie really is here."

"No, honey. I know you'd love to have him here, but he's not."

"I can feel him rubbing against my legs."

Frightened, Edeline suddenly sat up. In the dark, Sunny could see she still wore the khaki shorts and blue tee shirt she'd been wearing the day of the kidnapping. Edeline caught up a small box of matches near the blanket. She was sure some animal had gotten into the shed in the dark with them. It might be a skunk!

"All right, Chip," Edeline said, trying to sound calm. "Don't move. I'll get us a light in just a second. Stay away from it. Don't touch." She fumbled for the candle.

"It's a cat, Mother. I know it's Whiskie. He patted my nose," Chip said. Just by being there, Whiskie had already planted hope and courage in Chip's mind. For children and cats are natural allies who share secrets of the heart. Whiskie spoke a language of comfort, and Chip heard it.

"Keep away, Chip. Don't touch it," cautioned Buffy, sensing the urgency in her mother's voice.

Edeline struck a match and touched it to the wick of the candle. Light flared in the shed. There, arching his back and rubbing lovingly against Chip, was Whiskie. "Ali Baba's Captain White Whiskers of Effingham!" exclaimed Edeline, who had always been partial to the Turkish Angora's formal name.

And then there was such a frenzy of rubbing and petting and purring and hugging that Whiskie thought his little cat heart would burst with joy.

"Oh, Mother!" shrieked Buffy, as she snuggled her cheek against Whiskie. "He's come all this way just to be with us!"

"He's my friend!" exclaimed Chip. "He's just the best friend anyone could ever have!"

Chip tried to hug Whiskie, but Buffy still had a hold of him. A friendly tug of war developed between the two children, with the black Turkish Angora being happily pulled two directions at once. Edeline came to the rescue, taking Whiskie in her arms. Both children jumped to keep petting him and bowled Mom and cat over together, almost knocking over the candle. They all rolled off the blanket and onto the dirt floor, where everyone got dusty and petted and hugged.

The loud purring and happy squeals of joyous welcome caused the dogs outside to begin another uproar. Happily Sunny knew the men would not come out of the house to investigate. He and Chicago Red had taken care of that.

"What's ark! bark! bark! going on bark! bark! in there?" Jugular yelped.

"Eat off his head! Eat off his head!" Markee Day Sod threatened through a narrow crack in the wall. Snap-Snap's jaws made a loud *clack! clack!*

At last Mister Backward could wait no longer. He jumped to the dirt floor and joined in the enthusiastic greeting, adding his own purrs to the celebration.

"Mother, there's another cat," Buffy said.

Edeline held up the candle for a better view.

"Mister Backward! It's Mister Backward! What on earth are you two doing here?"

"They've come to be with us, Mother," said Chip. Sunny could feel how much seeing the cats had lifted the humans' spirits. Everyone was so happy he knew they had been wise to come. But now it was time for Sunny and Chicago Red to go. While the cats and humans laughed and hugged and purred, Sunny and Chicago Red padded along the rafter and slipped out through the hole under the eaves.

They passed out over the dogs, who'd already stopped yelping. As they came down the chain-link fence and crossed to their friends in the weed patch, dawn cast a golden glow in the eastern sky. Everyone purred to see them back safely. They wanted to hear every detail of the happy reunion. After Chicago Red and Sunny eagerly told the story several times, everyone knew their long trip from Ridley Park had certainly been worth all the effort.

"They're going to be just fine," Lady Gloriana said as they all capered happily away from the kennel. "After all, they have the power of friendship."

Back in the puppy shed, the celebration slowly began to calm down. Curled upon Edeline, Whiskie purred so deeply his whole side moved up and down like a bellows. His silky, black tail, which almost hadn't stopped twitching since the adventure began, became placid and still. He let out a deep sigh of contentment and fell asleep in his mother's lap.

CHAPTER SIXTEEN

Differences at Dawn

"**I**'ve never been so exhausted. I plan to find a comfortable limb in Oak House and sleep for days," Sunny told Chicago Red as they made their way around the barn and headed back toward the river.

"Will you hang out here for a few weeks?"

"No. Just a few days. The rest of us have to get home to our moms. Whiskie's Mom runs the Christmas Cat Show. That's why Wolfgang Roach stole her: to keep The Show from happening. He seems to have succeeded. But we have to get ready for other cat shows. What about you? What do you plan to do, Chicago Red?"

The cats all passed single file across the driftwood bridge. They walked up the other bank of the river and came under Oak House.

"Well, I think I've repaid my debt to all of you. I'm thinking about spending some time up here, maybe look up an old friend."

"As to that, we all consider ourselves your friends, Chicago Red. Me as much as anyone. I'd like for you to come back to Ridley Park and be part of our society."

"The cat show thing, huh?"

"And why not? You've never tried it. Who knows? You might like it."

"I doubt it."

"Everyone thinks I'm to win 'Best of Show' this year. But you'd make tough competition."

Chicago Red got a twinkle in his copper-colored eyes as if enjoying the possibility.

"Wouldn't that be something? You and me in the same show. What are they like?"

"They're very exciting. And you have to be judged, which means you have to go to a table where a judge lifts you up and turns you around and pulls you this way and that to look at all your good points and bad points. Then he makes a decision. If you're good enough, you win a rosette. Your moms are all proud of you. It's loads of fun."

Chicago Red rolled his eyes to the lightening sky. "I'd never be able to speak to my *Meena-Ooma* again."

A little anger flashed in Sunny. He was trying to let this stubborn moggie know he was welcome in Ridley Park, and that was no small honor. But he didn't seem to want it.

Sunny said with disgust, "Your *Meena-Ooma* is a pain in the butt, did you know that?"

"Oh, now watch what you say, Sunny. Maybe I was a little clumsy in turning down your offer, for which I apologize. But you're walking on sacred ground now. So careful, my friend."

They stopped near the trunk of Oak House and waited their turn while the other cats climbed into the big oak tree. Hildy led the way up.

"When we first met I was disappointed you didn't have a secret name. Now I ask, Why was that? The secret name meant a lot to me. Why did you have to make me question my beliefs?"

Chicago Red started up the trunk of Oak House. Sunny followed close behind. "Because your *Meena-Ooma* is not your ambition, Sunny. It's far removed from all ambitions."

"And then there's my wild voice. That was so natural I didn't even know I had used it. It's like purring. No human knows why we purr. But we do, and all cats do it." And, in fact, Sunny was right: scientists don't know why or how a cat purrs.

"You're right. We purr because of something inside us: our *Meena-Oomas*."

Sunny let out a long sigh. "Don't say things like that. What does purring have to do with *Meena-Oomas*?"

"Purring is your *Meena-Ooma* singing." Chicago Red found a broad, unoccupied limb and lay down.

"What do you mean?" Sunny asked, as he climbed a little higher and found a comfortable spot in the crotch of three limbs.

"Do you purr when you're alone?"

"No, I don't purr when I'm alone."

"I can't explain it exactly. But I once heard a poem that explains it. It was in *Owtic.* I'll say the translation for you. It goes like this:

The purr is the song of the *Meena-Ooma.*
It is the *Meena-Ooma* singing its life is right.
When the cat and its *Meena-Ooma* are one,
The *Meena-Ooma* sings a song of joy,

And this we hear as the purr.
It does not matter if the cat is sick,
Or feeling pain, or even dying.
The point is, at that moment
The *Meena-Ooma* is rejoicing
In everything being right
Between itself and Creator.

And this joy is beyond all comfort
Because it is comfort complete.
It is the peace of the *Meena-Ooma*.

In joy of being it sings.
In joy of being it purrs.
The song of the *Meena-Ooma*.

"That's lovely," Sunny said. "You'll have to say it for me in *Owtic* someday. Do you know much of the old language?"

"Quite a bit, actually. My mother taught me the words and some of the grammar. She thought it was important that I learn the old language. Treated it as sort of a family heritage."

Chicago Red's voice shifted. He was drifting off to sleep. "I know the language, but I don't know much about its history. I leave that up to scholars like the Duchess."

Sunny's eyes were getting heavy. He said sleepily, "Maybe we should pay the cats in the barn a visit. And forget about the cat shows. I am. Maybe I'll stay out here with you, and we can spend the whole winter with Gar."

It took Chicago Red a few seconds to realize what Sunny had said. Then his eyes snapped wide open. He looked sharply up at his golden friend. How did Sunny know the name of his old friend and Name Keeper? Chicago Red knew he had never revealed the bear's name. How had this American Shorthair found out about that old tail winder? But there was no finding out now. Sunny was already fast asleep, and he deserved all the rest he could get. So Chicago Red stretched out comfortably on his limb and closed his eyes. Soon he was purring away in sleep, as Oak House swayed gently in the morning breezes in the warmth of the rising sun.

CHAPTER SEVENTEEN

An Awful Development

"Wake up, Sunny! Wake up! Something awful is about to happen!"

It was almost midday, three days after The Friendship had found Whiskie's Mom and her kittens. During these three wonderful days, Sunny had caught up on his lost sleep. He had also decided to rethink the name for his *Meena-Ooma*. Evidently there was more to naming his *Meena-Ooma* than he had thought.

"Wake up, Sunny! This is serious."

Sunny opened one green eye. Whiskie and Mister Backward stood with their hind legs on a limb just below him. Their forepaws rested in his nest.

"Ah," Whiskie said, spotting the single, lifted eyelid. "You're awake. Come on."

Sunny arose from the crotch of the three limbs. "You're interrupting important stuff: my sleep. What's the problem?" He stretched deeply.

The Scottish Fold chattered in confusion. Whiskie said, "My Mom is going to lead her two kittens in an escape."

"No!" Sunny exclaimed. "Why would she take such a horrible risk?"

"What?!" Gloriana gasped from a limb below Sunny.

"But that will put her kittens in danger!" Practical said in dismay.

"I admire her nerve," said the Duchess, "but not her judgment."

Everyone got so upset and talked so loudly, Sunny worried the noise would carry across to the house. "Shhhhh, everybody. The men could hear us."

More quietly, Mister Backward said, "They've got a plan all worked out."

"They've been saving bones and burying them under their blanket," Whiskie explained. "When they get six bones, Buffy and Chip will stick the bones through the cracks in the shed to distract the dogs. As they draw the dogs to that side of the shed, my Mom will lock the gates into the run in front of the big door. Once she does that, no dog can get into that run. The humans can dash out and escape."

"Will they do it tonight?" BraveHeart asked.

"Not tonight," Backward replied, shaking his Scottish Fold head. "They don't have enough bones. They need one bone for each dog."

"It will be a disaster!" Chicago Red exclaimed. "A dog doesn't grab a bone, lie down, and chew on it. One of the dogs will be bound to carry his bone to the side of the shed with the big door. When Whiskie's Mom steps out, he could maul her."

"They won't let the dogs carry the bones off. They'll wedge each bone in a crack. To chew on the bones, the dogs will have to stay put. That will give Whiskie's Mom time to slip into the run. Once she closes the gates so no dog can get into that run, they can escape. At least that's the plan."

"How many bones do they have now?"

"Three. They need three more."

"This is serious," Sunny declared. "We have to do something about it."

"What's the chance they'll escape safely?" asked the Duchess. She always liked knowing the odds.

"Poor," Whiskie replied. "They don't have our warm fur coats, and it's getting cold. They'll get lost. And where will they get food? Nowhere. They can't eat mice."

Chicago Red sprawled heavily over a limb, pondering the situation. "We could go with her and lead her back to Ridley Park. That way, she wouldn't get lost. But even then, the men could still catch her. And what if Wolfgang Roach sics those fighting dogs on her? They could seriously wound her or even kill one of her kittens. I see only one way out of this mess: I suggest we make sure she fails."

"I can't do that," Whiskie whined. "I can't go against my Mom's wishes."

"It's the only merciful thing," Chicago Red returned. "If those dogs can follow a scent, they'll be able to follow it day or night. They can run at a faster pace than the humans can. They'll catch them easily."

"*Can* the dogs follow a scent?" Gloriana asked.

"Maybe the cats who live here at the farm would know," Hildy offered.

"My thought exactly," Sunny said. "Haven't you and Gloriana been visiting in the barn with those cats?"

Hildy and Gloriana both nodded they had. Hildy added, "And the horse, Hudrughynhyn. He and Gloriana are practically old friends."

"Because I listen to his stories," Gloriana said. "Poor thing. He has no one to visit him, and he's very bad at telling stories. He makes them so long and tedious. Every story he tells starts with talk about the grass growing and the flowers blooming."

Gloriana's gentle patience with the horse's dull stories didn't surprise anyone. That was her way. It was one reason why both cats and humans were drawn to her.

Hildy added, "But there's something about these cats you all ought to know. My last time at the barn, a strange thing happened. I mentioned that we were show cats. They fell all over themselves being nice to me. They wouldn't hear of me sitting anyplace but in the warmest, most comfortable spot. And whenever I said anything, they listened with rapt attention, hanging on my every word. They even offered to catch me a mouse."

"Fame," Chicago Red said with a certain amount of disdain. "They probably think you're a very famous cat. You wouldn't believe how some cats act if they think they're talking to a famous feline. Perfectly ridiculous, but there you are."

For the first time concerning his opinions of show cats, Chicago Red found agreement among the cats from Ridley Park. They all thought such behavior certainly was ridiculous.

CHAPTER EIGHTEEN

A Question of Barn Cats

"Now just a tail-flipping minute," BraveHeart said. "Should we really tell these barn cats our secrets? What about the love between a cat and its mom?"

"A cat and its mom? Come on, BraveHeart! Surely you don't think the barn cats could possibly love those nasty men?" Whiskie objected.

"They certainly could. You know how loyal cats can be to their moms even if their moms are wicked. These barn cats might fight us. It would be dangerous to tell them our plans and have them support their moms the way we mean to help Whiskie's Mom."

"Good point," mewed Gloriana. She turned to Hildy. "What are these cats like? Exactly? How do they feel about the kidnappers?"

"That's hard to say," Hildy replied. "But BraveHeart is right. Some cats become strongly attached even to evil moms. They could betray us."

"How loyal could these cats be to those awful men?" Gloriana asked. "The men haven't even given them names. The idea of a name is alien to them."

"Why they sound worse than alley cats," the Duchess said snootily."They probably have no concept of trust nor any form of cultured behavior."

"Ah ah," said Chicago Red, measuring his words carefully. "Trust is not learned from being cultured, Duchess. Trust created civilization and, therefore, comes before culture. I've known alley cats more trustworthy than many purebred cats."

The Duchess paused for a second. She indulged in a little grooming to distract herself from her sudden embarrassment. Finally, she said, "I'm sorry, Chicago Red. I wasn't referring to you. As far as I am concerned, you have a pedigree as long as my tail."

"You can take your tail and stuff it up your nose and any pedigree along with it," the big moggie snapped.

The Duchess regarded him archly. "Naturally, I think we should treat these cats with all due respect. I'm merely saying that when a cat wants to get over a fence, she jumps on top first, then looks to see where she will land. A dog just jumps. I think we should all be cats and not dogs."

Rapidly changing the subject to stop the quarrel, Sunny suggested, "Hildy, why don't you go to the barn and ask the cats if we can meet with them?"

Hildy nodded and raced off toward the barn.

Whiskie said, "While the rest of you are talking to the barn cats, I want Gloriana to introduce me to this horse, Hudrughynhyn."

Gloriana looked surprised. "He'll tell you a long story that will bore you to death."

"I don't care. I want to meet him."

Hildy soon returned with good news: the barn cats were eagerly waiting to meet the show cats.

"Guess I'll tag along, too," Chicago Red said, casting a teasing sidelong glance at the Duchess. "Although why a bunch of gaga-eyed barn cats would want to meet a tacky, old alley cat like me, I wouldn't know." The regal white Persian frowned, but said nothing.

On their way across the river, Sunny noticed a definite chill in the air. Winter was coming on.

As The Friendship and Chicago Red entered the back door of the barn, The Tabby Cat was waiting to greet them. She led them inside, where three other cats sat on bales of hay. The bales were stacked unevenly and piled to the rafters, almost filling the room. To one side of the bales was a horse's stall.

A yellow tiger-striped cat, a black cat, and a calico cat all stood as the show cats entered. Although barn cats, they kept themselves clean. Their fur was bright, shiny, and healthy.

The Tabby Cat said, "Everybody, I would like you to meet some visiting show cats."

Introductions were awkward. But cats are at their best in awkward situations. Soon they were all settled at various levels on the bales of hay and chatting pleasantly.

"I'm sorry The Grey Cat isn't here to meet you," The Calico Cat said. "We're losing her, I'm afraid.

"Losing her? Where is she going?" Mister Backward asked.

"Oh, off everywhere. You know. Wild. I saw her from a distance yesterday in the meadow and called to her. She ran off through the rabbit brush. If she's going wild, I wish she'd run off into the hills. It's dangerous to be wild around here."

CHAPTER NINETEEN

The Friendship Makes an Alliance

"**D**o you know the men here well?" Sunny asked.

The Tiger Cat said, "We've had to get to know them. Our lives depend on knowing how to avoid them, especially Dakota and Beezley."

"Which ones are they?" Sunny asked.

"Dakota's got an empty, puffy face and hard, little eyes. He always carries a gun wherever he goes. Beezley's the tall, skinny, gaunt one. He looks like a cat that's been feeding on grasshoppers. Dakota caught The Black Cat and put him in a cage full of live snakes."

The Black Cat said, "But I got away and so did all the snakes. They're still living in the weeds around here. I hope one bites him."

"You could move if you wanted. Why stay here on this wretched farm with these nasty men?" Chicago Red asked.

"This farm has always been our territory and will be again someday," The Black Cat replied. The Calico Cat and The Grey Cat will soon have kittens."

"Really!" Chicago Red said. "Well, now, congratulations really are in order!"

"Thank you," The Calico Cat purred. "I only wish The Grey Cat were here to hear you."

The Black Cat thought a moment. Then he said, "They *are* nasty. To make fighters of the animals, the men have poisoned their food. The poison kills their gentle side and leaves only their brutal natures. That's what they did with the horse, Hudrughynhyn. But cruelty kills the spirit. That's what happened to their strongest, most experienced fighter, Top Dog."

Sunny recalled the old German shepherd with his listless despair. "To hear you talk like this is a great load off my mind," he said, "for I see you are not loyal to these men. We have business against them and would like your advice on a matter."

"We will be glad to tell you anything we know," The Tabby Cat replied.

"Very well then. This is the matter: We are here so Whiskie can comfort his Mom, who was kidnapped and brought here by those mean men. We've learned Whiskie's Mom is planning to attempt an escape. But we fear these vicious dogs. Can the dogs track their scent and run them down?"

"Yes, they can," The Calico Cat said firmly. "Those dogs can follow a scent well. Whiskie's Mom and her kittens can't possibly get away from them."

Chicago Red nodded. "We thank you, Calico Cat, for telling us this."

"*The* Calico Cat," corrected The Calico Cat. She shifted uncomfortably on the bale of hay, as if she felt uneasy correcting a show cat.

Still smarting from his quarrel with the Duchess, Chicago Red snapped impatiently, "That's not a proper name! That describes you. It doesn't name you."

"Um, well, uh, I suppose...all right! We know nothing about names. What should we call ourselves?"

Sunny quickly tried to smooth over the matter. "The Calico Cat is a perfectly fine name. In some naming traditions it would be an excellent name. It's just that where we come from, cats have a different tradition. That's what Chicago Red meant."

The Tiger Cat said, "Please tell us your tradition. We have no traditions here. None of us has ever been far from the farm. We're just so delighted to meet you all. We'd be thankful for whatever you can teach us."

"I'm sure we're the ones who will be grateful in the end," Sunny said. "What we can teach you isn't nearly as important as what you've just taught us." *And that,* Sunny thought, *is the truth.*

"My," said The Black Cat, "you show cats are so gracious. I feel like an old piece of harness leather. Do tell us your naming tradition. I'm sure it's lovely."

Sunny explained, "In our traditions cats have first of all a formal name, the name we are officially known by at the cat shows."

"Ah. So this formal name is the name of your fame?" asked The Tabby Cat.

"Well, yes. That's a good way of putting it. It sort of is the name of our fame. Then there's a second name, the name our families and all our friends call us."

"And that's the name of your friendship."

Sunny looked puzzled. Then he passionately nodded an agreement.

"Good again. My fame name is Heartland's Sun at the Morning of Manning, and my friendship name is Sunny."

Duchess HighMind said, "Tell them about the third name, Sunny."

"A third name?" asked The Tiger Cat. "You have *three* names?"

Sunny said. "Our third name is special. We choose it when we're old enough to know ourselves."

"And what is this third name the name of?"

Not wanting to get into a discussion about *that*, Sunny replied, "It's not so much what it names. It's just an old tradition with cats where we come from."

"This is very interesting," The Black Cat said. "Since The Black Cat is not a proper name, my friendship name shall be Blackie."

"And mine shall be Calico," said The Calico Cat, tilting her white head with patches of black and red.

Sunny saw the barn cats were excited about their new names. But he didn't want to discuss the matter any further and neither did his friends. So The Friendship and Chicago Red excused themselves and headed outside toward the field east of the barn to look for Gloriana and Whiskie.

We've learned a lot, Sunny thought to himself as they crossed the barnyard toward the pasture. *Most important, we now know the barn cats won't help the men and the dogs can track a scent.* As they passed under the barnyard fence, they saw the Russian Blue and black Turkish Angora far out in the high grass of the pasture, heading toward them. The cats coming from the barn altered their path to intercept their two friends.

CHAPTER TWENTY

Confessions of an Equine Warrior

They met far from the barnyard fence well out in the green pasture. The grass still smelled lush and pungent. The cats picked out spots in the grass and lay on their tummies.

Once everyone was settled, Sunny said, "The barn cats believe Whiskie's Mom has no chance."

"What if she could travel as fast as the dogs?" Gloriana asked.

"Then it might be okay. But she can't do that."

"Remember Whiskie's vision that she would escape on the back of a friend?"

"Yes. But none of us can carry her."

"What if the friend," Whiskie proposed, "were Hudrughynhyn?"

A general murmur of surprise went up from them all.

"We've told the horse how kind my Mom is to all animals. I told Hudrughynhyn that if he helped my Mom escape, he would never have to fight again. He says he'll do it. He's a mustang. Mustangs live in the desert and can run long distances without tiring."

"But he's a fighter!" Sunny pointed out. "Can we can trust him with the prisoners?"

Whiskie's reply was sharp and irritable. "I don't believe that's true at all. I think the men put that idea in his mind to serve their own rotten purposes. You thought my vision was false. But it wasn't. If you're true friends, you'll figure out how to make this work."

With that, he grumpily got up and moved off through the grass toward the kennel.

Gloriana said, "Unfortunately, there's a snag. There's no way we can make Whiskie's Mom go to the horse. We'll have to tell him when she's ready, and he'll have to run to her and present himself to be ridden away. But he'll be locked up. That means we have to figure out how to operate his stall door. We thought maybe the Duchess could hide tomorrow and watch the man who handles him. Maybe she can figure it out."

"Wait a minute," Sunny said. "I should like to talk to this horse first."

"That's easily done," Gloriana said. "Come with me." She led them all back to Hudrughynhyn. She explained, "When you say his name aloud, it sounds like a whinny."

"I am very pleased to meet each of you," Hudrughynhyn said politely after Gloriana introduced them.

"I'm told you're a mustang," Sunny said.

"Yes. I am," Hudrughynhyn declared. "A mustang, the envy of all horses, the great runners over wide open spaces, the durable and tough."

"Not to mention most modest," Practical giggled.

"How did these men manage to catch you?" Sunny asked.

"Well, let me tell you, the grass was growing one spring day in the desert, the rocks were crumbling, and if you've never watched a rock crumble..."

"Um, I don't mean to be rude," Sunny said, interrupting. "But we're in kind of a hurry here. Could we skip the grass growing and the rocks crumbling just this once?"

"Hurrumph!" the horse whinnied with a kind of irritated sneeze. "Well, all right. But you're missing some of the most interesting parts. Let's see, now. How did these men manage to catch me? Actually, they didn't. When I was wild, I made friends with a young girl and went to live with her family. These men took me from her father and brought me here. I was never captured. I had already surrendered my freedom to live with a friend."

"How did you come to be friends with a young girl?"

"Her name was Darling Sue, and she was in terrible pain. She could not walk and had to get around in a chair with wheels on it. Her father used to bring her into the desert and push her around in her chair. I lived in the desert as part of a famous herd. Darling Sue was always so brave and full of hope and light. But she was confined to her chair and could not leave it. I could never have been that brave and happy if I had to sit in a chair all day. I came to love her courage. Then one day some mean men came in trucks and chased my herd. They had long ropes they threw over our necks. The ropes were tied to heavy weights that slowed and exhausted the strongest of us. The men captured the horses who were too exhausted to fight anymore."

"How ghastly!" said the Duchess. "Were you caught by one of those ropes?"

"Yes. But my rope got tangled in some bushes. The men didn't see me. They drove away. But I was trapped. I was so frightened I ran this way and that. The rope got wrapped all around me. The next thing I knew, I was lying on the ground wrapped up in it. I stayed that way for two days and two nights before Darling Sue and her father found me. Darling Sue was so kind. They set me free and brought me water. Then they went away. My herd was gone. I was all alone. But Darling Sue and her father came back. I wanted to be near Darling Sue and hear her sweet voice and feel her soft hand. Darling Sue and I became dear friends. One day she begged her father to put her on my back. He seemed afraid, which was wrong of him. I would never have hurt Darling Sue. But she kept urging her father to let her ride me. I wanted to make her happy. When he finally put Darling Sue on my back, I took great care to make sure she didn't fall off. I tell you, we had a wonderful time that day. I carried her everywhere, and she laughed so much tears rolled down her cheeks. After that, she came back to see me a couple of times. Then one day she and her father showed up in a truck. I was afraid of that truck. But Darling Sue wouldn't let me be afraid. With her coaxing, I got in the truck, and they took me home with them.

"What a wonderful life we had at her father's ranch. Then one day she stopped coming to the barn to see me. Shortly after that, Darling Sue died. For many days, I was very sad. I cried and cried. But to conclude my story, some men came to the ranch. They looked over all the horses. They seemed to be good men. So Darling Sue's father sold me to them. But they weren't good men at all. They were Wolfgang Roach and his crew. They brought me here, and I grew angry and hostile. To be honest, I don't remember hurting a single horse. But these men say I have hurt many horses, and they know much. So I must have."

"That's baloney!" Chicago Red said explosively. "I don't believe you've hurt a thing. The real you is kind and gentle but very strong. The barn cats told us the men put poison in your food to make you hostile and angry. Stop eating the food they give you. Eat only the grass here in this field."

"But winter is coming on. This grass will be covered with snow. I'll starve."

"Don't worry," the big moggie said, "By winter, Whiskie's Mom will have escaped, and you'll be far from this evil place."

"In a few days she'll escape, and so will you," Sunny told the horse. "We'll tell you when."

As the cats crossed the field and headed toward Oak House, Sunny mewed to Gloriana, "You were right. He is a gentle soul. I can't think of anyone to whom I'd sooner trust Whiskie's Mom and her two kittens than to Hudrughynhyn. That was a very sad story about Darling Sue."

"I wish you hadn't been so rude when he started talking about the grass growing," Lady Gloriana replied. "He does so like to talk about that, not to mention the rocks crumbling."

"I think it's good he's going with us," BraveHeart said. "Poor Hudrughynhyn. Even with the stuff Wolfgang Roach and his men feed him, he'd probably try to make friends with any fighting horse he met. Where does that awful man get the idea he can turn Hudrughynhyn into a killer?"

Suddenly, as the barnyard fence came within sight, a great uproar began at the kennel. The dogs barked and growled furiously. The men shouted and yelled. And in the middle of all the hullabaloo came the frightened cry of a mortally wounded cat: Rowroar-ro-OOOW!!! The wail was so terrible to their tender ears they froze in place. All their hackles went up.

"To the kennel, boys! To the kennel!" Chicago Red shouted. "They're doing something awful to Whiskie!"

CHAPTER TWENTY-ONE

Sunny Sees Top Dog's Despair

A crowd of rough, angry men burst out of the kennel run. Dakota carried a dead cat by the tail, its head pointed down. Sunny saw blood dripping from the cat's nose. The poor little creature's fur was gravely mauled around its stomach, and its soft underbelly was smeared with fresh blood.

The dead cat wasn't Whiskie. In fact, Sunny had never seen this cat before.

"Why, that's The Grey Cat," exclaimed Calico, who had just come to the weed patch.

It was obvious who had killed her. Top Dog stalked stiff-legged after Dakota, sniffing at the carcass.

Sunny inwardly raged. Top Dog was ten times the size of Grey Cat. The poor little thing didn't stand a chance.

As soon as the excited men retreated toward the house, Chicago Red crossed the barnyard toward the chain-link fence behind which Top Dog lay.

The big moggie's ears were rotated. Laid-back ears mean a cat's angry. Rotated ears send the message, "I have no fear of you and need to protect nothing." Chicago Red's ears plainly told Sunny the big moggie was going into battle without remorse.

Sunny ran to catch up with his friend. He wasn't about let him go to that fence alone. The two cats stopped at the fence. Top Dog ignored them and licked blood from his lips.

Chicago Red growled, "You must be terribly proud to have behaved so cowardly."

Top Dog rested his chin on his paws. He shut his eyes and muttered wearily, "I'm neither proud nor ashamed. I feel nothing."

"Then you're a cold-blooded murderer."

"I don't even feel cold-blooded, kitty. Cold-blooded would be something. There is nothing inside me — a nothing that comes from nothing and grows to nothing."

Sunny realized Top Dog must have fought too many times and killed too often. Death had infected his mind.

Chicago Red curled his lip. "You loathsome beast. How did you become so evil?"

Top Dog lifted his chin from his paws. He looked straight at Chicago Red. His eyes were like a burned-out car Sunny had once seen, an empty, charred hulk of cold metal. Now he understood what Top Dog had meant. Nothing was consuming him. He was being swallowed up by a vast nothing inside himself.

The cat has extraordinary nerve fibers that can transmit impulses at amazing speeds. In a lightning-fast move, Chicago Red thrust both forepaws through the chain-link fence. He hooked his left claws into the right side of Top Dog's face and his right claws into the left side of the dog's face. The German shepherd did not even flinch. He just lay there, staring with his icy eyes. Silently, Chicago Red pulled Top Dog's head closer and closer.

Top Dog continued to lie still, putting all his strength into his neck muscles to keep his head from being pressed against the fence. Unbelievable to Sunny, the big moggie was the stronger of the two. Slowly, relentlessly, he crushed Top Dog's head against the fence. The German shepherd's left ear popped through the links. Chicago Red bit the ear hard and hung on. With a little jerk of his head in the direction Dakota had just retreated with the corpse, Chicago Red said through clenched teeth, "She was to have kittens soon."

Top Dog just kept licking the blood off his lips. He smelled heavily of death and carnage. Then Sunny heard Top Dog mutter an odd encouragement. He said, "Kill me if you can, kitty."

Just then Snap-Snap and the two other dogs rounded the corner of the shed and set up a hullabaloo. Sunny knew the men would be there any second with their guns.

Fearing for their lives, the American Shorthair wedged himself between Chicago Red and the fence. Using all his strength, he broke the big moggie's hold on the German shepherd. Hastily, Sunny shoved Chicago Red toward the weed patch where The Friendship and the barn cats were anxiously waiting.

"Can we hide in the barn?" Sunny urgently asked Calico.

"Come with us -- quickly!"

Just inside the open barn door, in front of Hudrughynhyn's empty stall, Sunny and Chicago Red paused.

"Phaugh!" Chicago Red coughed, pawing angrily at his mouth. "I'll have the wretched taste of that beastly dog in my mouth for days."

Sunny could see Chicago Red was still raging with anger over The Grey Cat's death. He wanted to sink his teeth into something. He needed serious distracting.

Suddenly, Sunny had an idea. Sitting down beside the big moggie, he said, "I think I know why you call everyone 'little fellow.' That's what your Name Keeper called you. You picked it up from him."

Chicago Red cocked his head curiously. Sunny could see this had distracted him and set him thinking.

"Gar! You've met Gar?" he suddenly exclaimed. "I knew it the other night when you mentioned his name. But I forgot all about it. Where? Is he still here?"

Sunny felt pleased with himself. Chicago Red was always surprising him and the other cats with startling revelations. It was fun to turn the tables on his large friend for once.

"I met him the first night we got here."

"Well, you certainly keep good news to yourself. How is the old tail winder?"

"Fine. But I don't think he wants to see you. I got the idea he's avoiding you."

"Avoiding me? Now, no, Sunny. We're best friends. Why would he avoid me?"

"Gar's getting old, Chicago Red, and he knows it. One of his canine teeth is missing. He's beginning to turn grey. He gets food by scavenging in garbage cans. He admires you a lot. He doesn't want you to see him reduced so much from when you knew him."

"Well, now, that's the greatest pot of nonsense I ever heard. I love that old tail winder."

Sunny nodded knowingly. "He doesn't want you to look for him. He even asked me not to tell you he was around. So if you do look him up, go easy. Don't expect him to be the bear he used to be."

"Why, of course I'll go easy on him. I'll bet he's still a tail winder."

Just then, the rest of The Friendship decided the men were not coming out again, and it was safe to return to Oak House. They said their goodbyes to the barn cats.

As he lingered to watch the gentle Scottish Fold make his way from the barn to the kennel shed, Sunny wondered to himself, *Have Whiskie's Mom and her kittens collected any more bones? Our only chance is to put Gloriana's scheme into action: we need to open Hudrughynhyn's stall door. But can the Duchess learn how to open the door from the man who takes care of the horse?*

Now everything depended upon the brainy white Persian. They'd just have to wait and see whether or not she could release Hudrughynhyn.

CHAPTER TWENTY-TWO

The Duchess Brings Bad News

The next day, Sunny was up and out with first light, hunting for his breakfast. He covered the area under Oak House's wide, spreading limbs. This had been good hunting ground when The Friendship arrived. But nine active, hungry cats will hunt out an area quickly, and this morning pickings were slim. He made a meager breakfast on a little, fat wood mouse, then returned to his limb to doze away the day in short naps. By late afternoon, his hungry tummy would let him sleep no longer. It was no use. He'd have to venture out to the new hunting ground Chicago Red had found.

Just then, the white Persian climbed onto the limb beside him. "I have bad news," the Duchess mewed sadly. "I can't open Hudrughynhyn's stall door. There's a lever on the handle. To release the door, the human presses down on that lever with one toe of his forepaw. When I sit on top of the lower half of the door, I can barely reach the lever, and I can't budge it."

"What if two cats stood on the lever?"

"We tried that. It didn't work. We can't open the stall door."

Sunny tried to conceal his disappointment. "It's all right, Duchess," he sighed. "You did your best."

As the Duchess left to go catch her dinner, Sunny thought to himself, *What will we do now? We've exhausted every plan.* His stomach growled. *I'm so hungry I can't think straight.* He backed quickly down the trunk of Oak House and set out after the white Persian toward the new hunting ground.

The new area was situated in a grove of hickory saplings on a wooded hill not far from the farmhouse. He hurried in the golden, late-afternoon sunshine toward the grove. After he made a fine meal on two fat field mice, his gloom lifted. He sauntered back to a spot where he thought he might find the Duchess, only to discover the entire Friendship had joined her. They were all lying around in a small clearing, a picture of satisfied contentment.

Suddenly, Whiskie came flying into their midst. His eyes were wide with fear, and his tail was bushed out like a scrub-brush. "Help! Come quickly!" he screamed. "Dakota has captured Mister Backward! He means to let Top Dog fight him!"

"What? Where's Backward now?" Sunny asked.

"Dakota and Beezley are holding him in the puppy shed."

"Come on,' Sunny shouted to the others as he raced away toward the kennels.

They had gotten no farther than Oak House when a loud ruckus sounded from across the river. First came an ear-piercing, terrified *yelp!* followed by a deep, guttural, snarling growl dripping with hateful anger.

YOWLP!

GROOWL!

WARAOO-O-O-W!!?!

"Down! Back!!"

Ka-POW!

Then all was silent.

In mortal fear, the cats raced across the driftwood bridge and hid in the barnyard weeds. They stared out in horror at the puppy shed. Dakota, the man with the ugly, puffy face and hard, cruel eyes, crouched in one kennel run. He leashed the bulldog Captain Blood. The bulldog jumped wildly, barking furiously. In the doorway of the puppy shed stood a squat, solid man with thick, course features and a heavy head of dark hair touched with grey.

"That's Wolfgang Roach," Whiskie whispered.

Roach's left arm hung limply under a ripped shirt sleeve soaked with blood. His right hand held a pistol. He stared hard at something or someone on the floor of the shed. His thick, red face was set in furious outrage. Suddenly, he raised the pistol and shot three times at the floor.

"That's where they took Mister Backward," Whiskie cried in his wild voice.

Just then Tabby emerged from behind the puppy shed and slipped across to the weeds where the other cats were secreted.

"They've killed Top Dog," Tabby reported.

"They've what?" Hildy cried.

"Dakota put your sweet-faced Foldie friend on the floor of the puppy shed and let all the pups come in to watch. Then Wolfgang Roach brought in Top Dog. But when the men turned Top Dog loose to attack Backward, the old German shepherd just stood there, staring mutely at the cat. Instead of attacking, Top Dog lay down! Roach got so furious he started kicking Top Dog. That's when the brute leapt up and went for Roach's throat. Roach barely had time to raise his arm to protect his face before Top Dog's fangs sank deep into his flesh. Roach worked his gun between him and Top Dog, and the gun made that banging noise. Top Dog never yelped or even whimpered. He just silently rolled over and died."

In front of the puppy shed, a tall, gaunt man with a lantern jaw led three leashed dogs back and forth across the ground. He pointed at the ground, urging the dogs to sniff the dirt.

"That's Beezley, Roach's assistant. He's trying to get the dogs to pick up a scent," Tabby said.

"*Whose* scent?" Chicago Red asked in alarm.

"Mister Backward's," Tabby replied. "During the confusion, your Foldie friend got away. He's escaped!"

Just then, the two dogs Jugular and Snap-Snap gave out long baying moans.

"They've got Backward's scent!" Tiger cried in a panic. Beezley unsnapped the leashes. The five dogs set out at a loping run across the valley floor toward the foothills.

Tabby shook his cream-striped head sadly. "Your friend doesn't stand a chance. He's gone the wrong way."

"What do you mean?" Sunny demanded.

"That way looks good, but it's not. Many rocks and gullies up there in the hills will force him along a dead-end path leading to the lip of a cliff. 'The Plunge of Despair,' we call it. I'm afraid Mister Backward's cornered! Before long, the dogs will have him at their mercy."

CHAPTER TWENTY-THREE

An Awful Development

"The Plunge of Despair?" Chicago Red asked. His red-and-white ears perked up alertly, his coppery eyes widened, and his whiskers splayed open in front of his face. "Is there a shortcut to that cliff?" he asked. His voice sounded strange.

"Yes, you can get there quickly. But why?" Tabby protested. "You'll only watch helplessly as those evil dogs force your friend over the edge of the cliff. The fall is as tall as five redwoods."

Chicago Red's firm chin looked even more determined. "Come on. We have to get there before they do. Show me the way."

"Okay. It's your hide," Blackie replied. "Follow me!" Only Whiskie stayed behind. With Backward in grave danger, Whiskie's Mom needed his comfort now more than ever.

Years later, when he recalled that race to the Plunge of Despair, Sunny could only remember splashing wildly across the river, then laboring through rocks and scrub brush until his chest burned with pain. The eight cats came out over the top of a small rise overlooking the brink of a great cliff. They stopped and hid in a patch of rabbit brush. With sinking hearts, they saw they were too late. Mister Backward, the men, and the dogs had already arrived. The red-and-white Scottish Fold was backed to the lip of the murderous cliff, facing five snarling dogs. Snap-Snap lunged repeatedly at Mister Backward, barely avoiding the Foldie's sharp claws. Behind the dogs stood three men, watching and shouting encouragement. Dakota's rifle rested loosely under his arm. Roach's pistol was holstered. It was clear the men thought the dogs could handle this pipsqueak of a cat with no problem.

"I'm going down to Mister Backward, boys," Chicago Red said in his wild voice. "You all stay here."

"You can't fight all those dogs by yourself!" Gloriana exclaimed with alarm.

Sunny was speechless. *Chicago Red has been acting funny all the way to this cliff top,* he thought to himself. *He's been preparing himself for some plan he's hatched. But what could it be?*

"I can't let the little fellow face those dogs alone," the big moggie replied. "But I'm warning you: don't any of you come with me. You boys need to get back and help Whiskie. He's in a plight, and no doubt about it. He needs you. You can't help me fight these dogs. Why, with all of us in there, we'd probably win. Then Roach would step in with his gun, and we'd all be killed. But I've talked too much as it is. I've got to do this before I lose my nerve."

"Lose your nerve to do what?" Sunny demanded. "What do you mean to do?"

"Never mind. Just don't try to help me. No matter what happens. If I don't live through this, Sunny, watch for Gar and remember me to him. I'd sure love to see that old tail winder one more time. Tell him I'll be waiting for him in *Malowando*."

With that, Chicago Red bounded down the slope, his ears rotated and his large red-and-white tail lashing. He crashed through the dogs with a fierce gnashing of teeth and scratching of claws. The dogs pulled back in yelping surprise. Before they could regroup, Chicago Red shot through them toward Mister Backward. That's when Chicago Red made a dreadful mistake.

Exactly what the mistake was, Sunny couldn't tell. Chicago Red's footing must have slipped. Or maybe he meant to stop and turn, but he was going too fast. In any case, Chicago Red crashed pell mell into Mister Backward, striking the Foldie broadside. Mister Backward never even saw his bi-colored friend coming. Chicago Red rammed into the tiny Foldie with all the forward motion his huge weight had generated as he dashed down the slope. The Scottish fold's slight frame lifted off the ground and sailed like a leaf over the cliff. The two cats at first clung to each other, in a sort of midair hug. Then each fell separately, making a long, heart-dropping plunge through empty space down, down, down many heights of trees. Both cats disappeared into the treetop foliage at the foot of the cliff far, far below.

At the top of the cliff, the dogs and the men froze, dumbstruck. They silently stepped forward and peered over the edge. The drop was so far that no man or beast could possibly survive the fall. The men muttered to each other. They were just about to kill that little cat with the folded ears. Then poof! he was gone. A second cat, a real giant, had crashed down the hillside and knocked the little cat off the cliff. Was the second cat a friend or a foe of the one they'd cornered? Somehow, the two cats seemed to know one another. Ah, well, it made no difference. Instead of one dead cat, now they had two. They leashed the dogs and headed back toward the farmhouse.

CHAPTER TWENTY-FOUR

The Friendship in Mourning

The Friendship and Blackie slowly made their way back to Oak House in subdued silence. The burden of their tragic loss left them numb. In the blink of a cat's eye, two dear friends had been taken from them. No one knew what to say. No one knew what to do.

Sunny was sick with anguish and sorrow. The big moggie had knocked the Foldie off that cliff on purpose. That much was clear. The bi-colored tom they'd all come to love had given his own life to save Mister Backward from a painful and humiliating death. But, oh, why did it have to be this way? Try as he might, Sunny could think of no good reason. The image of Mister Backward and Chicago Red, locked together plummeting to their deaths, hurt fresh each time he recalled it. A terrible, empty heaviness hung leaden on his soul.

Back in Oak House, the cats of Ridley Park lay still under a clear, starry sky. They barely moved. Numb with grief, they gave little more thought to Whiskie's Mom and her kittens.

On the second day following the tragedy, the prisoners received meat for dinner. They got another bone. They now had four. They needed only five.

On the third day following the tragic fall at The Plunge of Despair, as the sun dropped over the western edge of the world, Sunny woke up. Practical was jumping from limb to limb through Oak House, singing a rollicking song:

The sun woke up this morning, took your snoring
  as a warning
That you'd bite him if he made you come awake.
In dread he chose to hover,
Fumbling for a cloudy cover,
While your snoring made the whole creation shake.

Now we linger in this shake up, and the world can't
  get a wake up
'Cause the sun in trembling hides its yellow face.
And it's really getting boring
As your rumbling, fearsome snoring
Keeps the day from coming to its proper place.

Of course Practical did not mean morning. She meant evening. But the song was originally written by a day person — not a cat.

"Go away, Practical," Hildy groused. "We just want to be left alone."

"Let's go hunting," Practical replied. "You need mice to eat. We have a mom in serious trouble. If our two lost friends could see you now, Mister Backward would be mortified and Chicago Red would be furious."

Just as Practical pondered whether to turn some of them out physically, a mewing and meowing floated up from below. She peered down and saw the barn cats at the base of the tree.

"Can we come up?" Calico asked.

In a few moments, they were settled on limbs, and Calico was setting forth a proposal. She said, "We've all decided to use some of your names as our secret names."

"I'm going to be Sunny," said Tiger.

"And I'm going to be Hildy," said Calico. Her stomach was getting round as it was near her time.

Gloriana shook her head, "No, no, no. You can't do that!"

"You don't want us to use your names? But we admire you so, we want to be like you."

Hildy smiled gently. "You just can't tell everybody your secret names. The secret name is sacred. Only you and your Name Keeper can ever hear it."

"What's a Name Keeper?"

"The cat who makes your secret name into a real name. If you keep a name to yourself, it takes on a feeling of a fantasy after awhile. So to make it a real name, you tell one other cat: your Name Keeper. Neither of you ever mentions the secret name again."

"Would you be our Name Keepers?"

"Of course. Once asked, no cat can honorably refuse to be a Name Keeper."

"Good," said Tiger. "Then you're all our Name Keepers and we can tell you our names. I'll be Sunny, and Calico will be Hildy. Blackie will be Whiskie, and Tabby will be Practical."

Hildy and Sunny exchanged looks that seemed to say, "I don't think they've got it, do you?" And, "Oh well, let it go."

"Is that all right?" Tiger asked.

The cats from Ridley Park felt they'd like to get off this subject.

"That's just fine," Gloriana lied. "Really wonderful. You've got it just right."

"It's not quite right," the Duchess put in, giving Gloriana a warning look. "I'll explain it more to you later."

After Calico and her friends left, Sunny observed, "I guess they certainly do admire us."

"And don't you feel ashamed of yourselves for lying around moping?" Practical said. "Can you imagine how disappointed those hicks would be if they ever learned you let Mister Backward's and Chicago Red's deaths get the best of you?"

"I wish you wouldn't call them hicks," Sunny said. "It's wrong. They're decent, and they're on our side. Hick sounds, I don't know — bad."

"How about barn cats, then?"

Sunny accepted that and dropped the subject. Before they headed out to their new hunting ground in the hickory grove, Sunny went to the barn and invited the barn cats to come hunt with them. The barn cats seemed flattered by the invitation. Together the barn cats and The Friendship happily hunted the night away.

CHAPTER TWENTY-FIVE

A Lecture on Deep Matters

The word *Malowando* bothered Sunny. Chicago Red's last words were:"Tell Gar I'll be waiting for him in *Malowando.*" But where was *Malowando?* Early one morning while Sunny was finishing breakfast in the new hunting ground, the Duchess came to the clearing in the hickory grove and stretched out on a sunshine-warmed rock. Sunny crossed to her. "Duchess, have you ever heard of *Malowando?*"

"Certainly. *Malowando* is an *Owtic* word that means 'the place where cats are perfect.'"

"And where's that?"

"It's not a place anywhere in this world. Most cats believe it's where we go when we die."

When we die!?

Those three words made it final. Chicago Red *had* known he was about to die. And yet if the big moggie had been right, if his *Meena-Ooma* was more real than his teeth and claws, maybe somewhere –right now – Chicago Red was still alive.

Sunny looked thoughtful. "Duchess, would you teach me about the *Meena-Ooma?*"

"Of course. I've been giving the barn cats a few short lectures on secret names. As moon-luck would have it, tonight I'm going to explain the *Meena-Ooma*. Why don't you come?"

And so it was that late that night, when all the men in the house were asleep, Sunny found himself in the barn, surrounded by barn cats. Hudrughynhyn was in his stall.

The Duchess lay on her stomach, taking her ease on a bale of hay above her students. Her brilliant-gold eyes looked wise. "*Meena-Ooma* is an old *Owtic* word. *Meena* literally means 'only self' and has the '-*ooma*' suffix attached to it. '*Ooma*' connoted great respect in the old language. So *Meena-Ooma* could be taken to mean 'the self which is unique and special.'"

"But what *is* the *Meena-Ooma* exactly?" Sunny asked.

"That's a good question, Sunny. The *Meena-Ooma* is a plan, or a pattern, Creator put inside you. It's who Creator meant you to be. But because you have free will, this plan has no authority. Creator gave you the ability to learn, so you can find and recognize your true pattern, your true self. Once he finds his *Meena-Ooma*, or true self, the correct cat names it, thus making it real. Because this true self is deep, it must be kept in the deepest part of the mind. It can't be discussed openly."

As Sunny mulled this over, Hudrughynhyn went crazy in his stall, snorting, prancing, and spinning.

"What's wrong with that horse?" the Duchess asked impatiently.

Sunny swiveled his golden ears. "Something – or someone – is outside the barn, headed this way."

Listening intently, Blackie said, "It's that bear, the one who prowls around the garbage cans at night."

As Sunny's green eyes turned toward the open door, a bulky shadow appeared. With a deep, guttural grunt, the bear lumbered into the barn. He headed straight toward Hudrughynhyn.

It was Gar, all right.

"What's wrong with you?" Gar grunted at the horse. Though he may have meant to sound soothing, his voice was a rumbling growl. The terrified horse reared, snorted, and kicked.

Sunny leaped up between the two animals and perched atop the stall door. "Hello, Gar."

"Sunny! What are you doing here?" Gar grunted.

"What did you want with Hudrughynhyn?"

Gar swayed his massive head back and forth. "Chicago Red told me I should show this silly horse I won't hurt him."

That can't be true, Sunny thought to himself. *Chicago Red's dead. Why would Gar lie to us?* For certainly Gar *was* lying. Sunny knew the bear hadn't seen Chicago Red before he fell over The Plunge of Despair.

"And why did Chicago Red say that?" Sunny asked, trying to sound casual.

Gar didn't answer. Instead, a deep voice just outside the barn door answered, "Because Gar can tear off Hudrughynhyn's door and set him loose so Whiskie's Mom and her two kittens can ride to freedom."

All the cats in the barn recognized that voice. They happily turned their eyes on the open door just as Chicago Red, followed by Mister Backward, stepped into the barn.

CHAPTER TWENTY-SIX

The Friendship Is Made Complete

They were all so surprised they totally lost their cat poise. "Mister Backward! Chicago Red!" they cried.

And "Is it really you?"

Gar lay on the dirt floor and rolled around while the cats tumbled over him. (He was careful, of course, not to hurt the "little fellows"). Meanwhile, Hudrughynhyn thrust his great neck over his stall door, placing his head in the middle of the action. "But how is it possible?" "I don't understand!" "Didn't you fall over the cliff?" and "I know you did! Are you ghosts?"

The cats couldn't take their eyes off Mister Backward. Something about him was different. Sunny suddenly saw what it was. "Your ears have straightened out!" he exclaimed. "They're not folded anymore."

For it was true. Mister Backward now had upright, pointed cat ears, just like any other cat. The fall from The Plunge of Despair had scared his ears straight!

"Do you like your ears like that?" Tiger asked from his unusual perch on Gar's head. The other barn cats sat between

Gar's hind feet, which lay splayed out on the barn floor in front of him.

"No, I don't," Mister Backward complained. "Now I look like any other cat. And that fall from the cliff taught me I am *not* just like any other cat."

"We'll just have to get to know the new you," Sunny mused. "We're all changing, you know. Why, even Gar and Hudrughynhyn have forgotten their differences."

The others looked at the bear and the horse. Hudrughynhyn still had his neck over the stall door and his head down at cat level. Gar sat next to the horse's head, with his foreleg casually laid along the horse's neck. Gar patted him lightly. The fear vanished from Hudrughynhyn's eyes, and he whinnied happily.

"Tell us about the fall!" Practical exclaimed.

Chicago Red winked at Mister Backward. "You tell them, little fellow. I want to watch their faces."

"Simply put, it's just another of those impossible things we cats can do," Mister Backward began. "Chicago Red and his mom used to live in a far away city where people lived in very tall apartment buildings. Every spring when the windows were opened, a few cats would fall out and get injured or killed. But, amazingly, some cats who fell weren't hurt. One day, one of Chicago Red's friends, a little spotted cat named Freckles, fell a frightful distance — the height of many, many trees—and landed without harm.

"Her mom took her to the vet, and the vet said Freckles wasn't the only cat to have fallen that far without getting hurt. Cats often do that. The vet said the Animal Medical Center in New York had once looked at 132 cases of cats who'd fallen out of high buildings. Amazingly, 120 of the cats survived. One cat survived a fall of thirty-two floors. If a cat falls, say, three to ten stories, the cat will almost always get hurt or die. But cats who fall from a great height will frequently walk away healthy. The vet also told Freckles' Mom about an eight-year-old Siamese named Cognac, who plunged 1,100 feet from the wheel cover of a light plane and scampered off unharmed into the woods. Of course, not all cats live through a great fall. But many of us do. Nobody knows why."

Chicago Red added, "I always remembered that Animal Medical Center study. When Blackie told me how high The Plunge of Despair was, I figured maybe we could live through it."

As he listened to this astonishing story, Sunny happened to glance at Gar. The bear didn't even seem to be listening. *Why is he so blasé?* Sunny thought to himself. *It's such an amazing tale that even if Gar has heard it a hundred times, he should still be fascinated. Unless, of course -- he knew all along Chicago Red could fall that far and not get hurt.* And Sunny suddenly knew the story they were still telling around the campfires up here. Sunny almost blurted it out before he remembered this was connected with Chicago Red's *Meena-Ooma* and was, therefore, wrapped up in the feelings of privacy a cat has about his secret name. So he listened patiently and held his tongue.

"But even knowing about that study, Chicago Red, weren't you afraid to jump off that cliff?" Practical asked.

Chicago Red nodded. "It took me all the way from the puppy kennel to The Plunge of Despair to get up my nerve. Throwing yourself and one of your best friends off a cliff, boys, is not easy. I hope you never have to do it."

"Only a true and courageous friend could have done it," Sunny said solemnly. "And I think I speak for everyone here when I say this: Chicago Red, you've shared our dangers. Will you share our glory? Will you become a member of The Friendship?

The moggie humbly replied, "Boys, I may not have been a member of The Friendship, but you've treated me as friends should. And I'll just say, yes, and thank you for asking."

So Chicago Red joined The Friendship and went through all the cat things one has to go through when joining such a special club.

"As my first act as a member of The Friendship," Chicago Red said, "I want to give a certain cat here a new name. Obviously his old name no longer fits him."

"But what will his new name be?" Sunny asked.

Chicago Red paused to let their curiosity build. Then he said, "From now on, he shall be known as Mister BoldFellow."

And so Mister Backward's friendship name was officially changed: he became Mister BoldFellow from that moment on.

CHAPTER TWENTY-SEVEN

A Change of Plans

Sunny and Chicago Red walked with Gar out to the rabbit-brush-spotted meadow behind the barn. They came to the place where the bear meant to strike out toward his den. No path went that way, and there was no map. The three pals stopped in the chill night air under the arch of stars.

"I don't know how much longer it will be before we need you to open the stall door," Chicago Red told Gar. "I'll come for you when it's time."

"Don't make it too long, little fellow. I might go to sleep for the winter. It's past my time now."

As the bear turned to go, Sunny impulsively asked, "Is it true, Gar, that Chicago Red once saved your hide?"

Gar nodded. "To save my life, Chicago Red drew men and hunting dogs onto his trail. Then he threw himself off a very high cliff."

And promptly named his Meena-Ooma, Sunny thought to himself.

"So The Plunge of Despair wasn't the first time you've jumped off a cliff?" Sunny asked.

"Believe me," the big moggie replied, "every time you jump off a cliff, it's the first time." And that, of course, was the truth.

Gar said, "Thank you, Sunny, for knowing more than I do what I needed and for telling the little fellow," and here he indicated Chicago Red, "that I was around."

"It was my pleasure, Gar. Besides, I wouldn't have missed for anything hearing someone get away with calling the little fellow here," indicating Chicago Red, "the little fellow."

This seemed to tickle Gar immensely. Chuckling to himself, the old bear struck out alone through the low rabbit brush toward the hills to the east. As the two cats stood watching him go, Sunny said, "The plan Whiskie drew up, with Hudrughynhyn carrying his Mom to freedom and us showing them the way home, won't work."

"Why not?"

"Hudrughynhyn will be carrying three humans on his back through rugged mountain country. That mustang may come from a race of horses used to rough land. But I've never heard of horses who were mountain climbers. The dogs are fast and sure-footed. You saw how fast they are. They beat us to The Plunge of Despair even when we used a shortcut."

Chicago Red agreed, "True."

"My guess is that Hudrughynhyn can stay ahead of the dogs from here to Owl's Roost. But he'll lose ground from Owl's Roost to Three Falls. After that, from Three Falls to The Road, the way is treacherous with no trail. Before Hudrughynhyn can get out of these hills to The Road, the dogs will catch him along with Whiskie's Mom and her two kittens."

"What will we do? I can see by the glint in those green eyes of yours that you've got a plan."

Sunny regarded Chicago Red carefully, taking his measure. Then he said, "Whiskie's Mom can escape with her kittens only if we fight the dogs to slow them down. We have no other choice. It's either fight the dogs, or let Whiskie's Mom and her kittens get caught and possibly mauled."

Chicago Red looked solemn. "We need to talk this over with the others."

"Immediately," Sunny agreed.

CHAPTER TWENTY-EIGHT

Duties Assigned

After The Friendship had agreed to a cat to fight the dogs, Sunny said, "We'll use three guides and run them in relays." The leaves around them in Oak House were beginning to turn bright yellow. Soon the limbs on which they sat would be bare. Everyone listened intently as Sunny sketched out his plan. "Four of us will leave early this evening. One of us will wait at Owl's Roost, one will wait at Three Falls, and the other two will continue on to The Road. We need to send two cats on to The Road. None of us should travel through those hills alone."

"Why post anyone at The Road? What's their job?" Gloriana asked, flicking her long, tapered, blue-grey tail.

"As soon as Hudrughynhyn reaches The Road, the two cats posted there will run back along the trail to wherever we're fighting the dogs to let us know the prisoners have escaped. We'll then break off the delaying fight with the dogs and try to escape ourselves."

"What will the rest of us be doing?" Hildy asked. Her large, almond-shaped, green-gold eyes were wide and curious.

"This plan has two missions," Sunny carefully explained. "First, there's the Escort. We need three escort cats to go with Hudrughynhyn and lead him to The Road. Second is the Rear Guard: they'll stay behind on the trail and fight the dogs. Some of our roles, of course, are already decided. Whiskie has no choice. His Mom will naturally want to take him with her on the horse. Because it was my idea, I'll be one of those in the Rear Guard, fighting the dogs. Chicago Red has agreed to stand with me. But we still need to decide who will carry out the rest of the two missions. Any ideas?"

"You said we'll need one cat to guide Hudrughynhyn from the farm to Owl's Roost. I suppose stamina is the most important criterion here," Hildy mewed.

"Stamina and a level head," Sunny agreed. "Whoever guides Hudrughynhyn to Owls Roost will be running in the dark with a huge, heavy horse coming on fast just a few paces behind."

"I think Practical should be the one for that job," Hildy said. "She may be seven-years-old, but since recovering from that owl attack, there's something new about her: she's become more powerful and strong. And she's quite level-headed."

Practical purred at the compliment.

Sunny nodded. "Good. I agree. Whoever runs the second leg of the relay from Owl's Roost to Three Falls will need almost as much stamina but will also need empathy. The second escort cat will have to sense Hudrughynhyn's pace and keep him running at that speed. It seems to me that fits Gloriana to a tee."

Hildy nodded. "Of the three of us with the most stamina, that leaves BraveHeart to run the anchor from Three Falls to The Road. Which works out just right because on that stretch the men and dogs will be their most desperate to catch Whiskie's

Mom. We'll need an escort who's bold, fearless, and full of derring-do. I think you'll agree that's BraveHeart exactly."

"But which two of us should wait at The Road?" BraveHeart asked.

"They must be patient and swift. When the time comes to fly back and alert the others, they must be able to do it quickly. The Duchess and Mister BoldFellow would be perfect."

No one disagreed.

"And since I'm so big and strong, I'll stand with you and Chicago Red in the Rear Guard to hold back the dogs," Hildy volunteered.

"Perfect," Sunny replied. "Then I guess it's settled. Those to go with Whiskie's Mom as the Escort will be Practical, Gloriana, BraveHeart, Duchess HighMind, and Mister BoldFellow. Whiskie, of course, will be on the horse.

Just then the barn cats, minus Calico, climbed into Oak House and presented themselves to the council.

Tabby seemed to be their chosen spokescat. "We want to help with the escape," she said firmly. "This is our chance to strike at these men and stand up for justice. We willingly put ourselves under your command."

"Thank you, Tabby," Sunny said. "We accept your generous offer. But since you know nothing of the route to The Road, you can only help in the Rear Guard. That will be dangerous. You could get killed."

"We're willing to risk that," Tabby said bravely. "These are the men and dogs who killed Grey Cat. We have wanted to drive them from this farm for a long time."

"Then I guess that settles it. There will be seven of us in the Rear Guard," Sunny said.

"Excuse me," interrupted Tabby. "But only three of us from the barn can help you. Calico had her kittens last night. We can't expect her to leave them."

"Well, why didn't you tell us sooner?" Sunny asked. "This is good news."

"Would you like to come see them?" Blackie asked.

The Friendship hurried to the barn. They found Calico tucked away in a tunnel at the back of a stack of hay bales near the horse's stall. In a small chamber deep in the tunnel lay seven adorable kittens piled warmly around Calico, who beamed up as each member of The Friendship peeped in for a look.

"Seven? But that's wonderful!" exclaimed Hildy. "I've never seen such a large litter."

"Yes," Tiger said. "We feel so blessed. It is, I think, a good sign. We barn cats now have even more to fight for."

CHAPTER TWENTY-NINE

More Than One Stroke of Luck

In the cold, black, pre-dawn hours, Whiskie's Mom lay quietly, listening to the dogs padding in the runs outside. Anxious about the coming escape, she had stayed awake all night. She was afraid that if she fell asleep, she wouldn't wake up before dawn. Their freedom depended on them getting a good head start.

Would all the dogs be distracted by the bones? What if one refused the bait? It could happen. Or what if one of the men in the house got up early and came outside? Unless she and the children moved ever so quietly, they would trigger an uproar of barking as soon as they moved away from the shed. Even if they escaped, Wolfgang Roach would put the dogs on their scent when he discovered his loss. But she had a plan for that.

She listened closely. Captain Blood, the part-bulldog brute, trotted by. His was a swift, prancing step. She had lived with these canine guards so long she could tell one from the other by their footsteps. Markee Day Sod had long, hard claws that rattled as he trotted, like someone shaking a silverware drawer. Jugular's trot was firm, solid, and hard. Of all the dogs, she feared Jugular most.

A shallow mountain river lay at the bottom of the gorge south of the barn. She had studied the river many times through the cracks in the shed walls. It appeared to run downhill and into the valley below. That meant it would show them the way out of these hills. As soon as she and the children escaped from this kennel, they would run to the river and wade along its course. No dog could follow their scent if they ran in the water. With some luck, the dogs might lose them completely.

Whiskie's Mom readjusted her position between the two thin blankets. She wondered how much time was left. She had no wristwatch. Roach had taken that long ago, stolen it right off her wrist. But she still had a way to tell when it was two hours before dawn. For the last two nights, at dawn, she'd checked the position of Jupiter in the sky. At dawn, the planet was about two hours above the horizon. As soon as Jupiter popped above the horizon, it would be time to flee.

How long has it been since I last checked the sky to see if Jupiter is up? she thought to herself. *Five minutes? An hour?* She had no idea. She quietly pulled back the blanket and stood. Crouching by the two sleeping children, she adjusted the blanket to make sure they were still covered. It was chilly inside the shed. She crossed her arms and briskly rubbed them with her hands to warm herself. Moving cautiously to the wall, she reached out one hand in the icy darkness until she touched wood. Pressing her face against the cold boards, she peered through a crack.

Her heart dropped like a leaden weight. A heavy overcast hung thickly above the hills. Not a single star was visible. The planet Jupiter would not be seen tonight.

She returned to the pallet on the dirt floor and sat down in shock. Why had she allowed the weather to determine their fate?

Whiskie came awake and crawled into her lap. Out of habit, she petted him. His purring, at twenty-six cycles per second (the same frequency at which a heavy diesel engine idles), soothed and calmed her. She leaned close and whispered, "What do you think, Captain White Whiskers? I'm sure it's well after midnight. Should we start?"

Whiskie looked up at her. In the darkness clinging around them, his large, almond-shaped, amber eyes gave her a long, slow copasetic blink.

Edeline said, "Okay, then. Let's do it."

She put Whiskie on the blanket beside Buffy and gently squeezed the little girl's shoulder.

"Buffy? Buffy?"

In seconds, both children were awake. Edeline lifted the corner of the shabby, thin blanket under which the bones were buried, and they all began to tear away the dirt with both hands. None of them saw a frosty grey, long-haired cat pass like a shadow in the rafters over their heads and disappear through an opening under the eaves. Hildy had been on this watch for the last hour and knew Whiskie's Mom had misjudged the time. It was only about an hour before dawn. She was getting a late start.

The three prisoners dug the last of the bones out of the earth and carried them to the wall facing the house. The dogs took the bait eagerly. Jugular was the first to grab one of the bones and try to work it out of the crack. Then Snap-Snap grabbed one. Then in quick order, the three young dogs — Captain Blood, Markee Day Sod, and Blood Hungry — followed suit. In no time at all, the five guard dogs were at the wall, chewing, gnawing, and tugging at the bones sticking out of the cracks.

Stopping to pick up Whiskie and one of the two blankets, Edeline crossed to the door. She opened the door and stepped outside. The dogs stayed on the far side of the shed, chewing on the bones, just as she'd planned. She paused for a moment and felt the icy, cold air on her face. A storm was brewing. Could they escape from these mountains before the storm hit? She moved to the gate, unlatched the hook that held the gate open, and tried to pull it shut.

The gate would not budge.

A shock of panic shot through her. For a moment she almost fled back into the shed. But her courage was strong. She tucked Whiskie and the blanket more tightly under her right arm and tried to think clearly. Why wouldn't the gate budge? The men must have lashed it open with some string or wire. With her left hand, she felt around the frame of the gate. At the upper left-hand corner, she found the wire, double wrapped, with the ends twisted together.

In a moment, she had the wire off and the gate closed and hooked. Now the dogs could not get at them. Just to be sure, she quickly wired the gate closed. She and the children were free to go.

Grateful that the dogs were still gnawing their bones, the three humans hurried silently through the thick dark toward the fallen-down barnyard fence and headed for the river beyond. Whiskie's Mom put out her left hand to feel for the fence as she walked. When her hand touched the wire, it felt hard, metallic, and cold. Just then, a horse trotted up from the direction of the barn and stopped in front of them.

"Watch out for the horse," Whiskie's Mom warned. She guided the children around the large animal and through a barnyard gate that hung off its hinges. They had gone several steps when Buffy, shivering in the cold and adjusting the second blanket around her small shoulders, said, "Mother, the horse is following us."

It was often said around Ridley Park, by those who watched her work with animals, that Whiskie's Mom could almost speak an animal's language. And in truth this was so. For animals do talk to all who care to pay attention. Just as a cat can tell you it's angry with a swishing tail or that everything is all right with a slow blink of its eyes, a horse can say "I'm safe and friendly" by the way it nuzzles gently and moves easily against you. The person who has a big and generous love for all things kind and faithful will find it possible to understand some deeply subtle and complex messages.

Still, Hudrughynhyn had to work hard to get his message across. They went through a ritual-like dance in which Whiskie's Mom led the children away from the horse, the horse pursued them and got in their way, and she shooed him off, only to find him a second later blocking their path and gazing at her with big, wistful, brown eyes. At last, Whiskie's Mom gently put out her hand to the horse, letting him sniff it. Hudrughynhyn touched her hand with his velvety nose, then turned sideways, once again offering the humans a chance to ride.

In a flash, they all mounted onto Hudrughynhyn's back. Chip sat in front of his mother, sharing a blanket with her. Edeline held the purring Captain White Whiskers. And Buffy, covered against the chill of the night with the second blanket, sat behind her mother.

"What a lucky break," Buffy whispered, as Hudrughynhyn started off at a slow trot. They passed the barnyard, then angled toward the high hill.

"Mother, he's not going toward the river," Chip pointed out.

"No," Edeline agreed. "But he's headed away from this awful place, and we can travel fast enough on him that we can be many miles from here before sun-up. Maybe we don't need the river. We've had a real stroke of luck."

"Goodbye, you cruel beasts," Edeline called, but not too loudly, to the dogs, who still had no idea the stolen humans were gone. She encouraged Hudrughynhyn with her heels, and the horse broke into an easy *clip-clop* trot. In the early morning darkness, marveling at their good fortune, Edeline caught no sight of a short-haired, brown tabby flashing along the trail ahead of Hudrughynhyn. She had no idea they'd been blessed with more than one stroke of luck.

CHAPTER THIRTY

The Rear Guard Takes a Stand

The Rear Guard left the Farm of Blood just after dawn under a heavy, threatening sky. As they crossed the meadow behind the barn, Chicago Red sniffed the air. A steady, chill wind reversed the lay of the long fur along his back, making it stand on end. "There's a storm abrewin', boys, and no doubt," he announced.

As they passed the kennel, the cats saw the shed door standing wide open. The dogs were silent when Whiskie's Mom and her kittens made their getaway, and they were still quiet. Unaware of the escape, the men remained inside the house. *So far, so good,* Sunny thought.

Ahead of them lay the hill they had to climb to get out of the valley. To Sunny, the hilltop looked much too far away. Would that he had the strength he'd witnessed Gar displaying just before dawn in the barn.

From the night they met, Sunny had been awed by Gar's size and strength. But he had no idea how strong the bear really was until he watched Gar release Hudrughynhyn. Gar simply rested one paw over the top of the door and braced his other paw against the stall. Then he ripped the stall door off its hinges as casually as if he were tearing a piece of tissue paper.

Hudrughynhyn reared and whinnied in panic. But Hildy spoke to him in the soft, soothing voice Gloriana had taught her to use to quiet the horse.

"Easy, Hudrughynhyn. Easy. Easy. Easy," Hildy chanted.

Gar looked down at the splintered door. "You know," he beamed proudly, "I feel a lot younger."

"Gar, you old tail winder," said Chicago Red. "You *are* a lot younger."

Gar put a huge, tender paw on Chicago Red's head, and the big moggie let the bear pet him.

In the following spring, the farmers at the bottom of the foothills reported a strange happening: many barn doors were ripped off in the night. Nothing was ever stolen. No animals were ever hurt. Just doors shattered, broken, and splintered. The farmers were mystified. But those cats who lived through the coming flight from the hills thought they knew the secret. And whenever they heard of another splintered barn door, they would fondly remember seeing Gar, standing over that shattered stall door, looking young and powerful again.

Climbing up the long hill, Sunny put his memories behind him. The duty of the moment posed difficulties enough. As they trudged up the hill, Sunny felt grateful to the barn cats for their help. At each switchback, he looked over his shoulder and was glad to see Blackie, Tabby, and Tiger trotting in line with the rest of the Rear Guard.

Reaching the crest of the hill, they set out at a snappy, silent trot. The narrow path wound through scattered oak trees, then meandered up and down hills. The snow began, and a white powder collected on the trail. Sunny's breath became labored.

His legs ached. *Oh, bother,* he thought. *It's hardly past dawn, and I'm already tired.*

They came out into the meadow where Chicago Red had driven off the owl that attacked Practical. Big, wet snowflakes, blown hard by a powerful wind, slanted across their vision.

Just when Sunny's legs grew so weary he had to stop for a rest, they heard the tracking sounds of the dogs. The dogs bayed in that long, excited way they'd sounded when they tracked Mister BoldFellow to the edge of The Plunge of Despair.

Moving at a quicker trot, Sunny turned his thoughts to Practical, Hudrughynhyn, and the rest of the escape party. *How are they doing?* he wondered. *It's too soon for them to be at Owl's Roost. Can they hear the dogs? If they can, are they scared?* He wished them courage and turned his attention back to the stony trail underpaw.

Much later that morning, the trail dropped between two hills into a narrow canyon, where it was lost from sight. The Rear Guard plunged into the cool shadows. Their only trail was a narrow path between a sheer rock wall on their right and a broad, crashing river on their left. No wind blew in the canyon. The air was warm. It smelled of ancient water and fishie things.

Far into the canyon, they came to the place Sunny remembered and was looking for. The trail along the river bank narrowed. Just where water and bank met, a large rock thrust up. A passage no wider than two cats lay between this upthrust finger of rock and the sheer canyon wall. The Rear Guard entered the passage, turned around, and sat down to wait. The narrow trail was like a gate at which the six cats could stand and refuse the dogs passage. To get around the cats and the rock, the dogs would have to enter the river, and the river here was deep and angry.

"Let's pray this storm stays as snow in the mountains above us," Chicago Red observed.

"If it changes to sleet and rain up there," said Tiger, "there'll be a danger of flash floods. Streams can go from little babbling brooks to raging rivers in minutes." Blackie and Tabby nodded in total agreement.

"We'll just have to chance it." Sunny said. "This is where we must wait for the dogs. In a place like this, we can hold the dogs all day."

"Not if the men use their guns," Chicago Red warned. "We'll have to retreat almost immediately if they do. Guns kill as fast as you can send a cat forward to replace the dead."

"I don't understand how those guns kill," Hildy said.

At these words, the Rear Guard fell silent. They tensely waited for the dogs to arrive.

Sunny wished Chicago Red had kept quiet about the guns. Everyone's spirits were low enough already. But he could do nothing about that now. So he sat and tried to be patient. The dogs came on relentlessly through the storm, baying low and adding an even deeper tone of melancholy to the cold, grey day.

CHAPTER THIRTY-ONE

Practical Leads the Way to Owl's Roost

Practical flashed along the river bank and through the canyon passage. Her four feet made a light, almost noiseless patter on the hard trail. Behind her, Hudrughynhyn's hoof beats echoed with a roar off the canyon's flat, granite walls.

As the brown tabby darted out of the canyon and began a long uphill pull, a rosy dawn filled the sky. Glancing quickly over her shoulder, she saw Hudrughynhyn galloping close behind her, his tail and mane flying in the pink-silver light. Whiskie's Mom sat upright, courageous and strong. Whiskie was pressed tightly against her chest, while Buffy peeked over her shoulder. In front, Chip held on for dear life, clutching fistfuls of the horse's mane in both hands.

By the time it began to snow, Practical was far beyond the canyon passage the Rear Guard would defend. The snow fell heavy and wet, melting as it hit the ground. White flakes clung to her short, dense, brown-tabby fur, then slowly melted, leaving her soaked.

Since taking flight from the farm in the pre-dawn darkness, Practical had not paused for a rest. She'd been chosen to run this leg of the escape because of her new stamina. This entire morning, she had lived up to The Friendship's trust in her. As soon as the escape party were settled on the dun mustang's back, Practical dashed away from the farm toward the steep hill. Hudrughynhyn followed her lead. At the top of the first hill above the farm, the brown tabby paused. The sound of Hudrughynhyn's hooves beating like hammers up the hill after her made her realize her danger. Suddenly, horse and riders thundered over the lip of the hill and loomed like a giant against the cloudy sky. A man is roughly fifteen times the size of the cat. Imagine, then, how awesome a horse and rider together must appear, and you'll see why Practical turned and raced away. In the face of death, her already tired legs were newly charged with courage.

Riding in front of his mother on the horse, Chip caught a brief glimpse of Practical flying along the trail ahead. "Look, Mother, Lady Practical is leading the horse," the boy said in breathless amazement.

The brown tabby was all but invisible on the trail ahead. "Yes, dear, keep that blanket wrapped around you. It's the only protection you have against this blizzard." Struggling to keep everyone on the horse, Edeline had no time to look for cats her children might wish were there.

Chip could see many things his mother could not see, like Santa Claus and the Tooth Fairy and the good angels who looked out for him and his sister. But that didn't mean Chip was imagining things. It just meant that even wise adults like his mother didn't always understand the really important things in life. "Go, Lady Practical!" he cheered their invisible guide.

Luckily, a cat has many resources to get across tricky terrain after dark. As she ran, Practical's whiskers became like a blind man's tapping cane *tap, tap, tapping* their way over the perilous land.

Practical raced across the clearing where Chicago Red had fought the owl to save her life. The horse's hooves pursued her without mercy. On through the early-morning darkness she sped. Running downhill hurt her legs with each jarring break of her forward motion. Running uphill exhausted her hind leg muscles. She sprang or tripped over rocks that scarred the tiny pads on her round, firm paws. Air whistled into her lungs as she gasped for breath. Her short, strong legs grew numb with fatigue. Still, she kept moving swiftly. She knew if she ever stopped, the horse could run her down by accident and cruelly pound her tiny body into the earth. The trail wound away from the river and climbed steeply uphill. It was a long haul. Her lungs burned for air before she was halfway to the top.

Earlier, before dawn, she had stepped on a pointy pebble. A sharp pain shot up her leg each time she put her weight on her paw. Now her whole left foreleg throbbed. Even so, she was so stout-hearted she kept up the pace. For, you see, the brown tabby had a way of running faster by stretching her backbone, which was held together by muscles. By lengthening her spine, she was able to increase her stride and hasten her speed without moving her feet any faster. That's another impossible thing cats can do.

For the rest of the trip to Owl's Roost, Practical ran in a fog. Later, she could not even remember seeing Gloriana waiting on the trail ahead to take up the second leg of the relay. In fact, Practical remembered nothing until she woke up hours later in a mound of muddy autumn leaves near a pile of owl pellets. A cold rain pelted down hard. Dogs yelped in the distance. Every muscle in her well-knit, powerful body ached. And yet she felt joyful. For at great peril to her life, she had led a fast horse for miles across a vast wasteland. And in the process she had learned a great lesson: what you can do depends not on your age or your size, but on your courage. Never again would she fret about her age when around the younger cats of Ridley Park.

CHAPTER THIRTY-TWO

The Rear Guard Is Sundered

The snow had changed to icy rain and was pelting down hard as Sunny and his friends stood in the narrow canyon passage, waiting for the baying dogs to arrive. The surging river was now full to the banks.

Five dogs came loping around the bend in the canyon, their noses to the ground, scenting the trail. Sunny and his friends lined up across the passage. Suddenly the dogs stopped, lifted their heads, and stared hard directly at the cats. That's because Chicago Red had surprised them all by bursting into song. In his deep baritone, he sang:

This is the line you have to cross
If one of you wants to get through.
But if you try, we'll give you a toss
Because we are the roaring crew.

The roaring crew, the roaring crew,
We'll fight you
And bite you,

Do all to spite you.
We'll give you a bump
And a mighty thump
While we kick your rump.
You'll be black and blue
If you try to get through
And come at this crew.

Growl, growl
We're on the prowl
To make you howl.
Howl, growl, howl, growl:
The howl of the roaring crew.

"Bark! bark! Out of our way!" Jugular ordered the cats. His eyes kept flicking back to Chicago Red. The soaked moggie greatly disturbed the black-and-white mongrel. Sunny suddenly realized why: Jugular was remembering that night in front of the kennel when they had made themselves invisible.

"You, bark, bark, guys again! Rarf! Rarf! I'm beginning to think you're not really, ark! bark! bark! stray cats! Out of our way!"

"We will not move," Sunny shouted firmly.

Captain Blood, the Russian-wolfhound creature, stopped near the edge of the bank. Apart from the others, he was alone and vulnerable. In a flash, Hildy shot at the young, inexperienced mongrel. Smashing into Captain Blood with her shoulder and all the weight of her Norwegian Forest Cat body, she flung him into the river. Rapidly swept away from the bank, the dog bobbed to the surface far out in the turbulent water near an uprooted tree. Swimming awkwardly, Captain Blood made for the tree and scrambled onto the trunk. Clinging to a limb, he headed rapidly downstream and disappeared around a bend in the river.

"Well, what do you know," Hildy said proudly, as she jauntily pranced back to her own battle line. "I seem to have chased a dog up a tree."

With barks, growls, snarls, and yaps, the dogs came at the cats in fury. An uproar of howls and hisses followed. Mud and water flew in all directions as the dogs and cats clawed, scratched, snapped, and bit. Suddenly, a piercing whistle rent the air. In response, the dogs whirled and fled back the way they had come. Far down the trail stood Roach and Beezley. No one else was with them. *Where are the other men?* Sunny wondered.

He had no time to worry. Looking down, Sunny saw he was up to his hips in water. What's more, the water over the trail was rapidly rising.

"Flash flood!" Tabby cried. "We're trapped. We're all doomed!"

Just then a great wall of water came roaring down the canyon. It washed over Sunny and his friends like a huge tsunami, sweeping them off the trail and downstream.

Sunny sputtered and gasped for breath. He struggled to keep his head above water, but the flood was too strong. Sinking under, he swallowed mouthful after mouthful of water. He fought back to the surface only to go under again. Just as he struggled upwards and burst into breathable air, he was sucked down again. It was like being caught in the rinse cycle of a giant washing machine. Once, as he rose to the surface, he glimpsed Chicago Red and Blackie, swept along by the current. They rounded a bend and vanished. Fighting for his very life, Sunny grew bone weary. The current battered, bruised, and drained him. He could no longer hold his head above water. Then he remembered what Chicago Red had said: "When a cat is in trouble he can call on his *Meena-Ooma*." He closed his eyes and spoke to his *Meena-Ooma*: "Oh, Unique and Special Self, be strong now. Be all Creator meant you to be."

With his eyes still closed, he let go and surrendered. The current was too much. He could fight no more. He dropped, unfeeling and unknowing, through the water until his feet touched the mud. The river's surface, he thought, must now be far above him. He was alone, deep, deep down in the river, on the mud bottom. He stopped holding his breath. Letting go, he gasped in the water that would end his life and release him from this unwinnable fight.

But Sunny did not gasp in water. What he breathed in was air. This shocked him so much, his green eyes flew open. To his surprise, he found himself standing in a little eddy pool at the edge of the flood. He had been washed ashore like a piece of driftwood. He glanced around. How far had he been carried by the water? He could not even guess. But he was only a few feet away from a gently sloping bank thick with shrubbery. He staggered up the bank and collapsed under the limbs of a concealing alder bush.

He was alive, but just barely. What had happened to Chicago Red, Hildy, and the barn cats? Had they been killed, their bodies swiftly washed toward the valley below? He had no idea. They were all hopelessly separated. Whatever the others' fates, alive or dead, the Rear Guard was now hopelessly scattered all along the river. Wolfgang Roach, with his vicious pack of dogs, his guns, and his brutal cruelty, was free to pursue Whiskie's Mom and her kittens however he wished.

CHAPTER THIRTY-THREE

From Owl's Roost to Three Falls

Gloriana had enjoyed several short naps before the exhausted brown tabby led Hudrughynhyn and his riders into Owl's Roost. Silently assuming the lead, Gloriana raced away toward Three Falls.

Well-rested and eager for this leg of the journey, the Russian Blue flashed along the trail, a small, silent streak through the sullen, grey day. The cold rain had turned the trail to mud. Behind her, Hudrughynhyn's flinty hooves continued to hammer hard on the trail. The horse had started to tire. But he great heart and endurance. He responded well to Gloriana's leadership, following any pace she set.

Gloriana was determined to keep up the pace. By now, they should have a good lead on the dogs. But they'd lose their lead on this leg of the journey if she failed to keep up the speed. So she set a fast pace. When she began to tire, she doubled her effort and tried to run even faster.

The wet snow had long washed away. The rain had turned the trail to slick, slippery mud. At Gloriana's back, an icy wind blew in gusts so strong they sometimes seemed to pick her up and boost her along. She flew along the trail, uphill and downhill, over rocks and fallen branches. The freezing wind pepped her up and made her run faster.

Until she heard the dogs, Gloriana had been very pleased with the race she had run. She knew the last leg of the journey, the one BraveHeart would lead from Three Falls to The Road, would be the toughest. That leg was all steeply downhill over soft dirt. There wasn't even a trail. It was on that stretch the dogs were most likely to overtake the escaping party. Gloriana ran so fast her legs ached and her chest burned. She could have traveled no faster. Yet even so, by the time she raced into Three Falls, she heard, over the roar of the crashing water, the baying of dogs. She also found BraveHeart waiting with bad news.

"The way ahead is washed out," said the seal point Siamese. His voice was calm, but determined.

"Washed out? Where?"

"Just below, at the foot of the falls."

"What are you going to do?"

"Find a way around it. It's a deep washout, and I don't think Hudrughynhyn can cross it. But it seems to get wider and shallower west of the river. I thought we'd travel along the washout until it gets shallow enough to cross. Those dogs worry me, though. They're getting close, and they don't seem to be on the trail. Do you suppose Wolfgang Roach knows a shortcut and has taken it?"

Gloriana's furry blue ears swiveled intently. "You're right. They're getting perilously close."

"Why don't you go take a look? That is, if you're not too tired. Maybe the dogs are chasing the Rear Guard, and you could help stall them." BraveHeart looked along the trail toward the bottom of the falls. "Needless to say, I'll need all the time I can get. Giddyap, Hudrughynhyn."

And with that, BraveHeart led Hudrughynhyn onto the trail. Gloriana sprang lightly to the top of a boulder alongside the rain-swollen river. From there she watched the fawn-and-brown Siamese cat and the dun horse pick their way carefully down the steep switchbacks by the side of the falls. From her perch, she could see the great, gaping fissure in the riverbank BraveHeart had told her about. He was right. That washout would take some negotiating. But she knew BraveHeart was up to the challenge if any cat was.

Her grey-blue ears pricked up. The barking dogs sounded frightfully near. Why were they already so close? She needed to check this out. Leaping down from the rock, she moved along the bluff over which the first falls spilled. At last, it had stopped raining. That made the going easier. But, even then, Gloriana knew the climb would soon become rough. She followed what looked like a deer trail through aspen and cottonwoods toward the crest of a hill thick with small shrubs. The barking dogs sounded as if they were just over that hill. Jarring gunshots suddenly split the air. Alarmed, Gloriana raced to the hill's crest, only to peer down not into a valley, but a dead-end canyon. Far below her stood a spreading sycamore tree. The tree was so close to the end of the canyon some of its branches brushed the canyon wall. Dancing all around the sycamore's thick, mottled trunk were all of Wolfgang's dogs, except Captain Blood. High in the limbs of the sycamore perched the entire Rear Guard. The cats stared coolly down at the frantic dogs. Twice, Jugular's mighty leaps almost reached Blackie's tail. But the limb on which the barn cat sat was just beyond his sharp fangs. Roach and his trigger-happy assistant Beezley stood some distance from the sycamore, firing their guns. To Gloriana's surprise, they weren't shooting at the cats in the tree. They were shooting at a silver streak of a cat, dashing in a zigzag pattern toward the sycamore. The guns made the wet dirt fly around the golden tom. In shock, Gloriana suddenly realized the tomcat was Sunny. The men fired their guns faster, as Sunny raced for his life. The murder weapons made evil sounds and sent the dirt flying in vicious spumes from under his gentle paws.

CHAPTER THIRTY-FOUR

Sunny Finds a Way

To understand how all the cats wound up in that tree, we have to go back to the moments when they pulled themselves out of the flood waters. But even before that, we have to go back and see what happened to Jugular. For after Jugular fought the Rear Guard by the river, he stopped tracking the horse. In his fury at Chicago Red, Jugular's nasty doggie mind zeroed in on only one thought: How could he find and kill the hated bi-colored tomcat? The men, of course, had no idea their prize fighting dog had switched from tracking Whiskie's Mom to tracking Chicago Red. The men and the other dogs foolishly followed Jugular.

In the flood, Chicago Red had loaned Blackie some of his great strength and both had been washed ashore. As the two cats stumbled through the woods, they heard the dogs baying behind them. Quickly realizing the dogs were pursuing him and not the horse, Chicago Red decided to lead the wretched mutts as far away as he could from the trail on which Whiskie's Mom and her kittens were escaping.

Unfortunately, Chicago Red had made a serious mistake. When he crawled out of the flood, the big moggie got his directions all turned around. In his confusion, he was actually leading the dogs directly *toward* the trail on which Whiskie's Mom was escaping.

In another part of the flood waters, Hildy had shared her Norwegian Forest Cat strength with Tabby and Tiger. The barn cats hooked their claws into the Weegie's long-haired coat and held on for dear life. Climbing out of the water, they headed west toward the trail where they soon encountered Chicago Red and Blackie.

"Am I glad to see you three!" Chicago Red exclaimed. As he and Blackie hurried down the hillside toward them, their paws sent loose pebbles flying. "Have you seen Sunny?"

"Afraid not," Hildy replied. "But where's the trail?"

"We're running away from it," Blackie said. "The dogs are chasing us instead of Whiskie's Mom. So we're leading them as far away from the trail as we can."

"Then I have bad news for you, my friends. You're not headed *away* from the trail. You're headed directly *at* it," said Tabby, who had an excellent sense of direction.

"Quick! The other way!" Hildy cried, reversing directions 180 degrees. She shot off up the valley. The others followed. To their chagrin, the cats quickly found themselves in a dead-end canyon. They discovered their mistake too late. The baying dogs were coming hard behind them. Trapped with no place to hide, the cats sped to the end of the canyon toward the trunk of a large, wide-spreading sycamore. Since up is hope to a cat, they scrambled up.

Meanwhile on another trail, Sunny was also following the sounds of the barking dogs. Weary in mind, body, and soul, he only knew he had to reach his friends. There had been only two men – Roach and Beezley–in the river gorge where the Rear

Guard was sundered. Where were the other men? Where was Dakota?

Following the yips, yowls, and growls of the dogs, Sunny arrived at a cliff overlooking a dead-end canyon. At the far end of the canyon stood a sycamore. To his surprise, Sunny saw his friends sitting high in the tree's branches as the dogs tore angrily around the trunk, barking furiously. Directly below Sunny, two men stood near a pile of loose rocks. With a sinking heart, Sunny saw both men had guns.

Frantic for his friends' safety, Sunny looked up and down the full length of the sycamore. His keen eyes spotted a footpath just behind the tree on the canyon wall. The footpath led from the canyon floor up and over the lip of the cliff. With one short, easy leap, his friends could land on the footpath, race up the cliff, and escape.

He called out to them in his wild voice: "There's a footpath just behind you. Jump!! You'll be free." But his voice was drowned out by the dogs' racket. None of his friends heard him.

I have only one choice, Sunny thought. *I must go to them. Even though it's certain death to attempt it, I have to race down the rock pile below, pass the men, and scurry up the tree.* The end of his tail began to flick slowly, then to lash rapidly back and forth. At that moment Chicago Red's words came back to him: *In times of danger, when a cat is being put to a test or is just unsure of himself, he may call upon his secret self, which will give him character and fortify him against all kinds of failures.* Standing alone above the men with guns, Sunny called in his wild voice for help from his still unnamed *Meena-Ooma.*

"Oh, *Meena-Ooma,* you who are the pattern put in me by Creator, be now as Creator meant for you to be. I tell you nothing. I give no advice. It is you who must tell me. It is you who must give advice. I listen with a hopeful and faithful heart, knowing that in this terrible moment, you will not fail me."

Erasing all thoughts from his mind, Sunny quickly leapt over the cliff and bounded courageously down the rock pile. Large, dislodged chunks of rock spilled toward the armed men with a great rattle and clatter. As he shot past the two men, Sunny instantly knew just what to do. He began rapidly zigzagging toward the tree. Bullets hit the ground all around him. Dirt flew up, spattering his fur, flying into his eyes. The cats in the tree saw Sunny sprinting toward them. They began cheering him on. But Sunny did not notice. He was running in the quiet of his mind. A great pool of elegant silence surrounded him as he ran. Even when a bullet kicked dirt up directly under his paws, he barely noticed. It felt as if someone had the earth on a string and had yanked it from under his feet. He flipped and fell. His friends' cheers turned to painful moans. But he was up at once running again, and the moans changed back to cheers. The men aimed and fired, aimed and fired. They missed, missed, and missed again. Time seemed to stop as Sunny fled across the wide canyon floor and shot up the tree among his friends.

Before anyone could speak, he shot out on a limb and leaped to the cliffside footpath. The other cats rapidly followed. They raced up the path and over the cliff rim to safety.

Looking back over the ledge, Blackie panted with relief. "Thanks to Sunny, we're safe. We've won!!"

Then a voice from behind them said, "No, we haven't won. Hudrughynhyn and his riders are only minutes from here. We must fight the dogs now to keep them from using this footpath."

At the sound of the voice, Sunny and the rest of the Rear Guard spun about to stare. Just feet from them stood Gloriana, staring back at them.

CHAPTER THIRTY-FIVE

Chicago Red's Last Stand

For the rest of the day, The Friendship held the path at the top of the cliff, and no dogs passed. The dogs came up the path, snarling and yelping. The cats met them at the top with hisses and spats. With teeth and claws, the cats drove the dogs back down the footpath where they would meet Wolfgang and Beezley. The two men leashed the dogs, calmed them, then released them and sent them back up the footpath to attack the cats.

In late afternoon, the storm clouds cleared away. The sun cast a dull, blood-red light over weary cats and dogs alike. Only Wolfgang and Beezley, cherishing their ability to inflict pain from a distance with their impersonal guns, remained eager for battle.

All the dogs were drained. Sunny and his friends lay gasping and panting at the top of the path, waiting for their attackers to come up again.

"Do us a great favor," Tiger said to Sunny.

"I'll do anything for you. What is it?" Sunny replied.

Tiger looked hesitantly from Chicago Red to Gloriana to Hildy to Sunny. He sounded embarrassed to ask for such a big favor. "Make us members of The Friendship."

"We certainly will, Tiger," Sunny smiled. "But it's not as great an honor as you seem to think. It's you who honor us by joining."

Tiger paused a moment. "It would be a great gift to us, Sunny. What you have done here, you have done for friendship alone. We admire that in you. We have taken it as our mission to tell The Friendship's tale to the whole wide world. Even if we do not return, Calico has sworn to tell her kittens your story. They will tell their kittens, who will spread the story of The Friendship far and wide. It is a great honor to become part of your legend. If I do not live through today, so be it. But I would like to die as a member of The Friendship."

They all went through the head-to-head greetings, saying the right things about honoring each other at all the right places. And with that, the three barn cats became part of The Friendship.

"But what about Calico?" Blackie asked. "She's not here to become a member."

"Why, then, we'll just make her an official member in *absentia*," said Gloriana, who had learned the word from the Duchess. It meant Calico could join, even when she wasn't there. "And while we're at it, we'll include all her kittens."

"Marvelous," said Blackie, who was so thrilled she was about to fly right off the cliff.

Chicago Red suddenly turned serious, "When Jugular gets up here again, don't fight him. Let him come through to me. Then close off the way behind him and go after the others. Rush

THE FRIENDSHIP CATS · 179

down the footpath and drive the other dogs back against the men."

Hildy protested, "You're going to stay up here alone and try to finish off Jugular by yourself?"

"I've got to," Chicago Red replied. "If I can do it, the other dogs might quit. It's our only hope. Here they come now."

In the dying light of the blood-red sun, Jugular stalked ahead of the others up the footpath. The Friendship moved to one side to open an avenue for him. He marched past them, aiming directly at his archenemy. Chicago Red stood calmly alone in front of the thick underbrush growing along the cliff edge.

In his wild voice, the big moggie said, "I relinquish control of this body, this battle to you, 'Faith-To-Fly,' knowing you will make no false step but act according to the true ways Creator gave you when he put you in me. Your will is my will. I trust in you." For Faith-To-Fly was the name Chicago Red had given his *Meena-Ooma* after jumping off that high cliff to save Gar.

Jugular approached Chicago Red with caution. He was more than twice as heavy as this cat; but unless he could make his weight work in his favor, it was of no advantage.

Meanwhile, Chicago Red eyed Jugular and made his own plans. He would have to move swiftly and certainly. But with his own powerful jaw muscles, his strong legs and back muscles, and his fast reaction times, he had a chance—if everything went right.

As the black-and-white dog circled him, Chicago Red spun around to keep facing his enemy. He flattened his body against the ground, trying to look as if he were preparing to spring. In reality, he was trying to tempt Jugular to jump and come down over the top of him.

As the noise from the battle below came up to Chicago Red, his antagonist sprang. Jugular leaped with both forepaws over the cat. Between those paws, Chicago Red struck like a bolt of red-and-white lightning.

Meanwhile, down the trail, Wolfgang Roach heard a cry from Jugular. Until now, partly out of fear of personal injury and partly from a desire to work up a blood lust in the dogs, Roach had held back from the battle. Now he forgot all his fears. In rage, he began clubbing at the dogs, forcing them to one side so he could rush to Jugular's aid. The dogs followed him. In a second, the men and dogs were racing up the cliff trail with the cats in hot pursuit.

But it was too late for Jugular. By the time Roach and Beezley reached the cliff top, Jugular lay lifelessly on his side with Chicago Red standing over him. Wolfgang's fury turned to cold, brutal hatred. He lifted the little, short-barreled pistol in his hand and stalked forward. Beezley cocked his rifle. Two men, guns raised, moved in on Chicago Red.

As the other cats came up over the rim of the cliff, they all plainly saw that Chicago Red's worst fears had come true. The humans with their guns had been drawn into the battle. The big tom turned squarely to face the men and their guns. Wolfgang stalked angrily, but calmly, toward the bi-colored tom. Sunny watched helplessly. Against those guns he could do nothing.

Suddenly, a great rattling came from the underbrush behind Chicago Red. A deep, snarling growl rumbled out of a cavernous throat as a huge beast barged through the thicket. Limbs popped and whole bushes snapped under a huge, lumbering weight. Now even Wolfgang heard it. Every hair on the back of his head stood on end. He turned toward the unexpected intruder. As Wolfgang stared in horror, right in front of him, out of the underbrush, reared up a huge bear. His head, shoulders, and great, hairy body towered over the brush, looming in front of Roach. The pitiful coward emitted a frightened, pleading whimper that died on his lips. Gar thundered toward him, snapping off bushes as he ran.

Realizing the puny gun in his hand was no match against a bear, Roach threw the pistol at Gar. But the bear just kept coming. Wide-eyed with fear, Roach and Beezley turned and fled down the path. Leaping and screaming in terror, they dashed pell mell down the footpath, scrambling away so fast no one could stop them. Sunny watched as the two men fled in terror with the dogs close on their heels. He realized they were of no more danger to him and The Friendship than a mouse. As Wolfgang and his assistant disappeared at the head of the canyon, hundreds of feet below, Sunny turned to Chicago Red and said, "You know, if we keep having adventures like this, I think I'd better try to find a mountain lion to be my Name Keeper."

The big moggie replied, "Or a bull African elephant."

Laughing heartily, all the cats rushed to give Gar a big hug.

CHAPTER THIRTY-SIX

The Battle at The Road

The sun was low and red on the horizon when BraveHeart escorted Hudrughynhyn and his three riders (four if you count Whiskie) over a little rise and saw The Road in the distance. Just the sight of The Road filled them with hope.

Whiskie's Mom and her two kittens were fast asleep on the brave little horse who had carried them so faithfully out of the foothills.

"Does this mean we've made it? We're free?" the mustang asked.

Without looking at his big friend, BraveHeart replied, "Maybe. Maybe not. I tell you what: I'll go on ahead to see how things look. You keep walking slowly. If everything's okay, I'll meet you at The Road."

And with that, BraveHeart took off like a shot toward The Road

As he ran through the red gloom of the sunset, the fawn-and-brown seal point Siamese tried to shake the feeling that something was dreadfully wrong. What could it be? The simple fact was, they did not yet have Whiskie's Mom and her kittens completely safe. So anything could be wrong.

BraveHeart's sapphire-blue eyes suddenly detected motion in the bushes just this side of The Road. He froze in place and intently studied the thick undergrowth. Just then, two cats emerged. It was the Duchess and Mister BoldFellow!

"What's wrong?" BraveHeart fretted. He felt only trouble could bring them this far out from their posts.

"Dakota and some other men are waiting for you at The Road," Mister BoldFellow said.

"With guns," the Duchess added.

"Let's go have a look," BraveHeart said.

The two sentries led BraveHeart to a stand of wild buckwheat at the edge of The Road. They looked across the asphalt at a black van parked just off the highway. Dakota was in the van with the radio on, listening to country music. He was smoking a cigarette. The front door of the van was open and Dakota's cowboy-booted left foot rested on the bare ground. His hard, little eyes in a soft, blank face studied the hills, searching for any sign of the escape party.

"Where's his gun? And the other men?" BraveHeart asked.

"The gun's on the seat beside him. Under his right hand. A bunch of hired men are all up and down the road. You just can't see them," the Duchess reported.

Mister BoldFellow said, "It seems to me this is the reason you were chosen for this leg of the journey, BraveHeart. We need a little derring-do to keep Dakota from going for his gun. Any ideas?"

"Yes. I can fix it so Dakota won't pick up that gun. He'll run from it."

Mister BoldFellow's deep-blue eyes stared at him in admiration. "If you can manage that, my friend, Whiskie's Mom will be free."

"Quick!" BraveHeart said to the Duchess. "Go back and get Hudrughynhyn and his riders. Bring them down here. Hide them from the van in that stand of poplar down the road. When you're all in place, tell Hudrughynhyn that he must wait until Dakota jumps out of the van. Then tell him to shoot across that road. Really fast. He must run as he's never run before. When he's all set to go, call to me in your wild voice."

The Duchess silently slipped from the stand of buckwheat and dashed for the hills.

"What do you want me to do?" Mister BoldFellow asked.

"Fight me."

The Foldie started to protest. But the seal point Siamese had already crept past the van and crossed the road to hide in a patch of rabbit brush. The Foldie quickly followed. Dakota sat listening to the country music, tapping his foot, unaware of the cats. They were now on the side of the road with the van, only inches from Dakota's boot-tip.

"I can't fight you. You're my friend," Mister BoldFellow whispered.

"I don't mean a real fight," BraveHeart whispered back. "I mean a pretend fight. Squawl and growl and scream at me."

"Okay. Then what?"

"Chase me. I'm going to jump in that van right over the top of Dakota. I want you to follow me."

"Jump into the car with that ugly man? No thank you. I'd just as soon not, if you don't mind." Mister BoldFellow was sure he hadn't become *that* much of a bold fellow.

But BraveHeart was firm. "This plan is our only hope. It's the only way Hudrughynhyn will be able to carry his riders to freedom.

"We have to startle him for just a second," BraveHeart continued. "If we make enough of a racket and create enough confusion, he'll want to get away from us. He'll leap out of the van. With luck, that will give Hudrughynhyn just enough time to escape to freedom."

Mister BoldFellow regarded him with large, thoughtful eyes. This hardly seemed to him like a foolproof plan. "What if he doesn't jump out of the car? What if he picks up his gun instead?"

"We'll be fighting over the top of it. No man, however dumb, is going to put his bare hand between two angry, fighting cats."

Just then the Duchess called to them in her wild voice. The horse was in place and ready to run.

Instantly overcoming his qualms, Mister BoldFellow let out a sudden scream so hideously frightening the fawn-colored fur on BraveHeart's back stood straight on end. Both cats shot for the van, their caterwauls filling the air. Dakota whirled in the seat. Fear flitted across his soft, puffy face. Both cats leaped into the van and across his lap, yowling and hissing. Dakota grabbed for his pistol. Before he could pick up the gun, BraveHeart sank his teeth deeply into the back of Dakota's hand. In pain, Dakota yawped. BraveHeart threw himself on the hard, cold metal pistol. He rolled onto his back, kicking and biting at Mister BoldFellow, who squalled like a wildcat.

His hand still smarting from BraveHeart's teeth, Dakota leaped out of the van in startled confusion. Suddenly, a loud crashing came from the poplar grove down the road. Dakota spun toward the sound just long enough to see Hudrughynhyn, a dun shadow in the gathering twilight, flash out of the bushes, their branches snapping back and popping as he passed. Then came the *cloppity-clop, cloppity-clop* of the horse's hard hooves on the asphalt. The riders clung on for dear life as the horse dashed across The Road, led by a long-haired, white cat.

Startled, Dakota took a precious moment to realize this was the escape party he'd been waiting for. They were galloping toward the woods where he was sure to lose them forever. Desperate to stop them, Dakota rushed back to the van for his gun. He stopped short. The two cats, now both standing side-by-side over the gun, arched their backs and hissed a warning at him not to come any closer.

In the distance, the sound of the horse's hooves changed. The mustang was no longer running on hard asphalt, but on soft earth. Dakota knew that in less than seconds his last chance to stop the prisoners would be gone, and the law would be after him. Ignoring the ferocious cats, he lunged for his pistol. For his effort, he got two paybacks: He got BraveHeart's teeth in his hand, and he got a bullet in the leg. Because Mister BoldFellow, knocked back by Dakota's lunge, accidentally stepped on the gun's trigger. The explosion right under the cats was the most frightening, most terrible experience of the whole day, and the shock to Mister BoldFellow's system re-folded his ears.

CHAPTER THIRTY-SEVEN

The Friendship Together Again

It was long after dark, somewhere on the trail between The Road and Three Falls, when the three cats from The Road met up with Gloriana, Hildy, and Blackie.

"Whiskie's Mom and her two kittens are free at last," Mister BoldFellow reported. "After they dashed safely past Dakota, we followed them just to make sure they didn't need our help anymore. I'm happy to say they quickly found a farmhouse owned by kind people who fed Hudrughynhyn and took care of Whiskie's Mom and her two kittens. The police came and even brought a trailer for Hudrughynhyn. So we left."

"That's great news! But what's this about Dakota being at The Road?" queried Hildy.

"He was there all right," the Duchess replied. "But Mister BoldFellow shot him."

"I didn't shoot him. I just stepped on the trigger. It was an accident," the Foldie protested.

But the other cats weren't about to underplay the adventure.

"You say Mister BoldFellow shot Dakota?" exclaimed Gloriana, her vivid green eyes dancing brightly. "That *was* bold."

"It was indeed," BraveHeart replied. "And, as you can see, the shock of the noise has re-folded his ears."

Mister BoldFellow stepped forward. The others were astounded: his ears were once again their old, folded selves.

"So now you look special again," Gloriana purred. "That's good because we all know how special you are."

"But what about the dogs and the men?" Mister BoldFellow asked, hastily changing the subject.

Blackie told them the whole exciting story. She concluded, "So now Jugular is dead, and all the dogs and men are gone for good from this part of the country. You can thank Gar for that. He couldn't have shown up at a more perfect time. He's in a cozy little cave in the hills above Three Falls. The others are there with him. We came down to find you and show you the way there."

They immediately set out for the cave. By the time they arrived shortly after midnight, Gar was asleep. Sunny and his friends were sitting out in front of the cave when everyone was reunited. The Friendship sat up the rest of the night, catching up on everything that had happened. They were especially happy for Mister BoldFellow and remarked again and again about his unique, re-folded ears.

Finally, toward dawn, they found comfortable sleeping places back in the cave. For the next three days, they slept almost nonstop, except for a bit of hunting and eating squeezed in now and then between naps.

For another week, they loitered about and retold their stories many times. For cats can never get enough of a good story.

The storm that had passed over these hills the day of the Great Escape marked the beginning of winter. One morning after hunting, Chicago Red and the Ridley Park cats were sitting inside the cave entrance watching an occasional snowflake blow by. Blackie, Tiger, and Tabby came in and gathered in front of their friends.

Blackie, who had been elected to explain, said, "Winter is coming on, and it's time to get back to the farm. Calico is there by herself with her kittens. She may need us."

"Yes," Chicago Red said, "we must be getting back ourselves. But it won't be as cold in the valley between here and Ridley Park as it will be where you're headed. We're not as pressed for time as you are."

"Thank you for everything," Tiger said.

"And thank *you* for everything," Sunny replied. "You did far more for us than we did for you. Without you, Whiskie's Mom and her kittens wouldn't be free today."

"Well, the men are gone now from the farm, and that was your doing," said Tiger.

"You know, of course, why we won, don't you?" Gloriana asked.

And in unison they all answered, "Because we have the power of friendship."

And they meant it.

CHAPTER THIRTY-EIGHT

Sunny Names His *Meena-Ooma*

It was several weeks later, having come back at an easy pace, that The Friendship spent a day and a night at Chicago Red's Safe House, the Place of Wrecked Cars.

"I can't believe you're the same cat who showed us this place so long ago," said Sunny, sitting in the sunshine between naps in the back seat of the same car they had slept in that first night.

"Oh, I'm the same cat all right," Chicago Red replied. "But none of you are."

Sunny put down the sparkling-gold forepaw with which he'd been grooming his ears. "Well, now, you're partly right. I know we're all different, and I think we've changed for the better." The Ridley Park cats all nodded.

"But you've changed, too," Sunny went on.

"How so?" the big moggie asked. He didn't believe he'd changed at all.

"When we came here that first night, you were a loner. Since then, you've joined The Friendship and walked many a trail with us. You're no longer the cat who walks by himself.

Although you're still the same independent cat you always were, you now have friends."

Chicago Red snorted. "You're show cats. I'm a moggie. There's a gap between us as wide as a river at flood time."

"Why not fully join our company and become a show cat?" Sunny offered.

"Impossible! I'm a moggie."

"You don't need a pedigree to enter a cat show, you know."

"House Pet or Companion division?" Chicago Red asked with disdain. He blew through his nose in derision. "Why I'd be constantly grooming myself with embarrassment. People are companions to me, not the other way around. No thank you, and forget it."

"Well, all right," Sunny conceded. "You'll remain our good friend and take an active part in our society."

"Oh sure, we'll start out that way. But I have my doubts it will last."

"None of us will hear of such nonsense," protested Hildy, who was sprawled on the back seat with Chicago Red. "You will always be my special friend, Chicago Red."

"We'll see," answered Chicago Red.

Their stay in Chicago Red's Safe House wasn't all naps, feasting on fat mice, and chatting with friends. Sunny also had some serious business to take care of.

Late that afternoon, he and Chicago Red hunted together near an old car's carcass that was missing windows, doors, seats, and almost everything else but the metal hull. The wood mice around the old hulk had an easy life. They were fat, lazy, and noisy. After eating well, Sunny and his old friend stretched out in the high grass and let the sun bake their fur. That's when

Sunny put his question to Chicago Red: "Would you be my Name Keeper?"

"I'm very pleased at the honor. But what about Whiskie?"

Whiskie is my good friend and always will be. But he spends his nights meditating on the moon. I know he will go far in wisdom, but he's no longer just right for my Name Keeper. He understands this and even suggested it to me himself while we were still at the farm. So I'd like you to be my Name Keeper."

"Then speak, and I will be. How will you call your *Meena-Ooma*, Heartland's Sun at the Morning of Manning?" Chicago Red asked in the formal way. For the naming of the *Meena-Ooma* is a very formal and weighty matter.

"Before our recent adventures changed us so much, I planned to call myself 'Champion' to honor my ambitions and my Mom's dreams for me. But no longer."

"And what is your third name to be?"

"*Wynnohm ! Ewm.* It's an old *Owtic* phrase the Duchess translated for me. I wanted to use an *Owtic* word to remind me of the long and broad tradition of our *Meena-Oomas.*"

Chicago Red nodded wisely. He knew the meaning of the words. He also knew that if Sunny had written the name down, as I have here, the ! is a symbol for a chirping sound that only Maine Coon cats can make without a great effort. Sunny had practiced silently for days to get the sound just right.

"Literally translated, your name means: 'My friends are my strength.'"

"It's a variation of Gloriana's phrase, 'The power of friendship.'"

And although Sunny, or Heartland's Sun at the Morning of Manning as he was formally called, never again spoke his secret name, he thought of it often and could be seen sitting alone in the sunshine or resting under one of the many backyard bushes around Ridley Park, meditating on the name of his *Meena-Ooma*.

That very night they made their way home through the back alleys. They followed the same route they'd followed when leaving the city so long ago. Near one side alley, not far from the cage in which they'd found Chicago Red, the big moggie made his goodbyes. "I'll be up to Ridley Park soon to see you all, and no doubt," he promised.

"You'd better make it soon," Sunny warned him. His green eyes looked fondly toward the Ridley Park Hills in the distance. "It's not very far, not nearly as far as we went for Whiskie's Mom. If you don't show up in the next few days, we're all coming down here to find you."

"If your moms will let you out of the house," Chicago Red quipped.

With his newfound confidence, Sunny easily replied, "Oh, I wouldn't worry about that, old friend. I do believe those days are over."

CHAPTER THIRTY-NINE

Home for the Holidays

It was in the wee hours of the morning when the Ridley Park cats arrived back in their old neighborhood. And what a surprise! It was the Christmas season. Every house twinkled with bright, festive lights, as if all Ridley Park was welcoming Sunny and his friends home. Red, green, white, and blue bulbs filled the night with a warm, friendly glow. It was good to be home at such a happy time. After walking about the neighborhood, relishing the familiar sights and the holiday smells of candy canes and cinnamon sticks, they saw it would be awhile before their moms were up and about. So they gathered under the lilac bush in Mister BoldFellow's side yard, where their whole adventure had started. The lilac bush had long lost its leaves, but the cats didn't care. They each found a cozy spot to lie under the lilac's bare branches.

"How do you suppose Whiskie's doing?" Sunny wondered aloud. He was eager to see his old friend, but he also knew things had changed between them.

None of them saw Whiskie for several days.

THE FRIENDSHIP CATS · 195

Later that morning, as she came out to pick up her morning newspaper, Sunny's Mom found the golden-apricot American Shorthair mewing at the back door. "Sunny!" Blair cried with delight. "You're home!" She swept him up in her arms, hugging him until he thought he would pop. "Jim! Look who's here!"

"Well, where have you been, you naughty cat?" Jim-Dad scolded Sunny affectionately as Blair carried him into the kitchen. "We were so worried about you."

"We must take you immediately to see Dr. Blaise," Blair-Mom fussed, as she opened a can of tuna fish.

That afternoon, Blair-Mom and Jim-Dad took Sunny to the vet. He didn't like the idea, but he knew it would be good for him, and he decided to put up with it. They were no more than settled in the waiting room when a big, bluff man came in with a red-and-white, bi-colored tom.

"Chicago Red!" Sunny exclaimed.

"Hello there, little fellow," Chicago Red said sheepishly.

"What a lovely Maine Coon cat," said Blair-Mom, stroking Chicago Red's heavy coat, which had been groomed to perfection, all silky and smooth. He smelled like fresh lavender. Sunny could now see that he'd been right all along. Chicago Red was indeed a striking cat.

"What kind of cat did you say he was?" asked his hefty, muscular "Dad," who was just as big a human as Chicago Red was a cat.

"A Maine Coon," Jim replied. "They are America's only natural breed. Some think they descended from cats who escaped from early sailors to America and interbred with the native raccoons, which is how they got their ringed tails. But that's a biological impossibility. A second legend has it that Maine Coons descended from Marie Antoinette's cats sent to

Wiscasset, Maine, when she was planning to escape during the French Revolution. Then there's a third legend and a real possibility: that they were brought here by early Viking explorers like Leif Erikson. That would make this big guy a distant cousin of the Norwegian Forest Cat. We have one of those in Ridley Park named Hildy. In any case, you've got a lovely cat there. Maine Coons are one of the most popular breeds in the country."

"He was a gift to me from the woman I'm going to marry. Trouble is, we're moving to England. It's not a good idea to try taking a cat into that country."

"Indeed, it's not," agreed Jim. "Did she give you papers with him?"

Chicago Red's "Dad" said, "Yes, she did. I just never paid any attention to them."

"Well, what do you know," Sunny said, walking over and sitting down by Chicago Red. "You have a pedigree. That means you can be entered in the Cat Show."

Embarrassed, Chicago Red quickly began licking his left shoulder. He looked up at Sunny with pleading copper eyes. "Don't tell any of the others, will you not, little fellow?"

The fact he and Sunny, for some unexplainable reason, seemed to know each other only made the Maine Coon seemed more adorable. Finally, Jim and Blair agreed to take Chicago Red home to live with them. The big tom's Dad promised to bring the papers by their house later that day.

So Chicago Red and Sunny saw the vet at the same time. Dr. Blaise pronounced them both healthy and unharmed. She prescribed only a few days of extra food and rest and lots of love to put them back in tip-top shape. Sunny's Mom and Dad then took both cats home and began grooming them for the cat show to be held just before Christmas. The cat was, as they say, out of the bag. Everyone in The Friendship soon found out that Chicago Red was a Maine Coon cat, one of the most lovable and most aristocratic cats in all America.

The Duchess, upon hearing the news, said, "Of course! That explains how he knows so much *Owtic*. Maine Coons are the only cats left who can make the chirps and trills necessary to speak the old high language."

"But I still say cat shows are a bunch of unmitigated nonsense," groused Chicago Red one day while The Friendship took their ease under the lilac bush in Mister BoldFellow's side yard. They were all there because Sunny had been right. Although most moms agree that keeping their cats inside is the correct thing to do, The Friendship had become a different bunch of cats. The moms of the Ridley Park show cats were never again able to make the inside rule stick. So they at last gave up trying.

"No, Chicago Red," Sunny said. "That's where you're quite wrong. Oh, no doubt, some things about our shows are superficial. But on the whole, cat shows serve us well, and I for one would not be without them."

The day was to come, however, when Chicago Red would not call the shows nonsense. Because in that year's Christmas Cat Show at the Gardens, when Sunny won "Best of Breed," "Best Shorthair," and "Best of Show" from all six judges and everyone in The Friendship won at least one rosette, Chicago Red himself took away a rosette as "Best of Breed." And that was no mean accomplishment for a cat whose Name Keeper was a bear.

Epilogue

No human ever knew the part The Friendship played in Whiskie's Mom's escape from The Farm of Blood. But this did not bother any of the cats involved. They knew if they'd been able to tell what had secretly happened, all their moms would have thanked them profusely. But they could not tell, of course, just as people who have the advantage of human speech cannot always tell their friends everything they've done for them. And that was fine with the cats of Ridley Park. They all enthusiastically agreed that friends never keep score.

None of The Friendship ever again saw Hudrughynhyn, but they heard plenty about him. From the moment the police arrived at the farmhouse from which Edeline phoned them after the escape, Hudrughynhyn was treated as a hero. He got his picture in all the newspapers and was hailed for his courage. Edeline had him checked out by a veterinarian, who pronounced him very healthy and "as strong as a horse." She then found the perfect home for Hudrughynhyn as a pace horse at a local race track, where he had his stall right next to all the glamorous race horses and soon become personal friends with some of the greatest champions in the country.

Gloriana, who had spent so much time on The Farm of Blood listening to Hudrughynhyn's stories, said, "No doubt he will be telling them about the grass growing and the rocks crumbling to dust."

And Gloriana was right. Hudrughynhyn did tell stories endlessly about nature's processes in the desert. But what she never knew was that those stories are interesting to horses. The horses at the race track, who lived a certain kind of disciplined life, could stay awake most of the night listening to the old mustang talk. And they frequently did.

Jim and Blair went on to become international judges at cat shows and later founded their own cattery. Eventually, being such experts on cats, Jim and Blair sold all they owned in Ridley Park and moved to South Africa, where they worked with authorities who were establishing a preserve for endangered leopards. They took both Sunny and Chicago Red with them, of course, and the two old friends lived out the rest of their lives exploring and wandering over a seven-million-acre game preserve.

Shortly after Edeline escaped and before The Friendship had made it back to Ridley Park, the police rounded up Wolfgang and his men. They were locked up in a human kennel and could not expect to get out while any of The Friendship was still left alive. So none of the cats ever again had to worry about those nasty men.

The easiest crook to be captured was Dakota. After Mister BoldFellow shot him, "by accident," as Mister BoldFellow kept insisting, Dakota tried to run away. The police caught him when he managed to make it to a doctor. He recovered nicely in jail while awaiting his trial. He went to prison, but there he experienced a transformation. After getting out, he spent the rest of his life running a shelter for homeless pets. But it was said that he liked cats best of all.

A year after their return to Ridley Park, Mister BoldFellow was spotted by a photographer at The Show, who featured him on the cover of *Cats* magazine. The response was so great that the adorable Foldie was given a full photo feature in the magazine. The publicity led to a contract with a famous brand of cat food and eventually to his own TV show.

BraveHeart, however, became the most famous of them all. Inspired by Mister BoldFellow's modeling career, BraveHeart's Moms opted for the movies for him. She placed him in the role of the companion to a globe-trotting adventurer. He proved so popular that he was signed to six more movies and finally given a life-time contract that provided him with all the tuna he could eat and a chauffeur-driven limousine. He spent his declining years hobnobbing with the Hollywood glitterati and was awarded a special Oscar at one year's Academy Awards as "The Cat That Has Done the Most for Hollywood."

Gloriana and the Duchess, after walking off for three years in a row with the most important rosettes at all the most important cat shows around the country, returned to The Farm of Blood after their moms urged Edeline to take them to the place where she'd been held captive for so long. All the humans were astounded to see a bunch of cats from the barn run to Gloriana and the Duchess, greeting them like old, lost, true friends, rubbing and bumping heads. Gloriana and the Duchess's Moms were at once taken by the layout of the farm. It would need a lot of fixing up. But they bought it and started an organic farm that became quite famous in that part of the country for its fruits and vegetables and for the best quality catnip in the nation. The barn cats were invited into the house, but they preferred their old barn. They were so good at keeping mice out of the vegetables and grains, however, that Gloriana's and the Duchess's moms loved them dearly and kept them well-petted and perfectly groomed.

Hildy's Mom went into politics and was elected to Congress five times. At first Hildy was left behind in Ridley Park. But her Mom missed her so much the Weegie was finally taken to Washington, where she established her territory at the Halls of Congress and became known as "The Capitol Cat." One new "independent" party took her as the party's symbol because cats always seem so independent (even though you and I secretly know how interconnected they really are). But the really good part was when her Mom was appointed ambassador to Norway. Hildy returned to the land of her ancestors and spent her remaining days hunting and lying in the sun, thinking about her secret name.

Whiskie became increasingly immersed in his quest for a mystical understanding of life. He, too, eventually grew tired of cat shows because he had to be groomed at times when he was meditating on the moon. He took off for Tibet, where he founded his own colony of contemplatives from among the stray cats in the streets. These cats, it was said, had a special air about them, and some of the local people began treating them as divine.

So, in the end, Whiskie spent his final years being idolized as a god, just as his ancestors had been in Egypt, back when cats could still speak *Owtic*.

With Love and Deepest Gratitude to:

Helga Browder, Rebekah Gilbert, Liz Mullen,
Mark and Stephanie Rohloff, and Robin Rohr
Carter, who kept saying, "I want to read the cat book."

ABOUT THE AUTHORS

A graduate of the University of Missouri, Walter
Browder (1939-2008) was a novelist, screenwriter, poet,
and co-author of *101 Secrets a Good Dad Knows* and
101 Secrets a Cool Mom Knows. Kizzy loved to purr on
Walter's lap as she told him this story. The third author
of this book, Mr. Cat, was his own boss, a cat who
adopted many moms and dads but refused
to be owned by anyone.

51874213R00122

Made in the USA
San Bernardino, CA
03 August 2017